BY THE BOOK

NEW OLYMPIANS ~ BOOK 1

C. J. VINCENT

Copyright © 2018 by C.J. Vincent

All rights reserved.

No part of this book may be reproduced in any form or by any electronic or mechanical means, including information storage and retrieval systems, without written permission from the author, except for the use of brief quotations in a book review.

PROLOGUE

Thousands of years ago, when mankind was young, they loved and feared the wrath of their creators. The Gods of Olympus reigned over their creations from behind a curtain of aloof power atop Mount Olympus. They were beautiful and untouchable; but they were also petty, cruel, and quick to anger, both with the humans they governed and each other.

The ruler of Olympus was known for his wild ways, and it was no secret that Zeus took female and male lovers whenever he felt his godly urges rising.

Zeus, Poseidon, and Hades, three divine brothers who were used to getting their way. But it was Hera, Queen of the Heavens, and wife to Zeus who finally had enough of her husband's philandering ways. When the appetites of their husbands were too much to bear, and the demigods grew too numerous to control, Hera, Amphitrite, and Persephone came together to protect mankind, and their divine bloodlines, by cursing the divine seed of their wandering mates.

Under the power of their curse, the Gods of Olympus could no longer impregnate humans, and their divine touch spelled death for their unwitting partners. When Zeus discovered what his wife had done, he was outraged. His anger split the heavens with divine lightning, but Hera's curse could not be undone.

With the help of his brothers, Zeus banished the goddesses from Olympus.

Zeus' immortal anger simmered for centuries, and as his half-divine children aged and died, he was left alone on Olympus with only his brothers for company...

CHAPTER 1 ~ HADES

A headache pounded behind my eyes. Maybe it was because we'd been alone for so long, but I was finding this new vision of Olympus to be more boisterous than I was expecting. Another shout of laughter echoed down the staircase. I flinched and sought the silence I craved deeper in my labyrinthine shrine to all the knowledge the world had to offer.

I inhaled the smell of my books and tried to force myself to relax. *Impossible, you fool.* I slid my book back into its place on the crowded shelf and trailed a finger through the thick dust that coated the dark wood in front of me. I glared at my finger angrily and swiped at another mound of dust that had gathered nearby.

When our marriage had been fresh, and Persephone had been eager to gain my favor, she would sometimes dust my library. When she first arrived for her six-month visit and was still filled with the vigor of summer, she glowed with the love her mother bore her, and she would be all too eager to please me. Those first weeks of our reunions were always sweet and wonderful, and I reveled selfishly in the pain it caused her mother, Demeter, to let her go. It would fade in time, that joy she had in seeing me, and by the end of her six months in the Underworld, I would be glad to be rid of her.

Her golden hair would fade to a dull brown, and her sparkling eyes would be hollow and angry. Our conversations, something I would look forward to with something bordering on eagerness in her absence, would change in that time as well—from interesting lighthearted banter to heated arguments over the smallest thing... It was as though Demeter wanted me to hate her daughter, and by the end of our six months together I would not argue or fight the decision that Zeus had made so long ago.

The goddesses always got their way. That much was true.

At least it had been... until now.

Zeus was the first of us to act upon the prophecy I had deciphered. The translation was not something I had done willingly or labored long over. If anything, I had hoped that it would keep Zeus occupied for a few more centuries... but he had found Cameron right away and wasted no time in his efforts to rebuild Olympus and spite Hera. I suspected that most of his efforts were fueled by his anger towards the goddess we once called Queen of Heaven. I even doubted that my younger brother had ever considered a deeper emotion than lust.

That Zeus, the Thunderer, could be faithful to any one being seemed preposterous. That any one of us could make such a promise... *could I?* I wiped another finger across another dust-covered book.

"What in Tartarus am I supposed to do about it?" I muttered aloud.

"About what?" A voice said from behind a shelf.

I smothered a yelp of surprise and peered around a stack of books to see Zeus' mortal... Cameron. He brushed his hair out of his eyes and smiled at me nervously. One hand rested on his swollen belly and the other reached out tentatively to rub across the thick spine of a book. The mortal was short and willowy, and the swell of his advancing pregnancy was impossible to ignore. He would be coming near his time very soon, which would account for Zeus' bold strutting. There was no doubt that Cameron was beautiful, and I could see why my brother had been drawn to him—but I supposed the young man's divine heritage had contributed to some of the initial appeal.

Cameron's skin glowed with health and his new divinity, and from what Zeus had told me, he seemed to have adjusted to life on Olympus well enough. But I had no patience for wide-eyed questions. I frowned down at him and tried not to smile as he swallowed thickly. Even though he was immortal, Cameron had retained his fear of the power he knew we represented. *Then again, everyone feared me. Whether they knew it or not.*

"What do you want?" I growled.

Cameron licked his lips nervously and pushed at his hair again. "I was just thinking that… well… no one ever comes down here and you might like some company."

"No one comes down here for a reason," I said sharply. Cameron flinched just a little and I smiled, knowing that the effect did nothing to soften my features. I had to be careful. If I scared the lad too much he would run to Zeus and I'd have to listen to my brother's lectures about welcoming the mortals all over again. He had already warned me to "lighten up" around them, but I don't think he really appreciated what a ridiculous request that actually was.

"Oh," Cameron said. He was silent for a moment, and I crossed my arms over my chest. "Can I borrow a book? I was in the middle of a class on *The Bacchae*—"

"I don't have it," I lied, cutting him off. Even though it made Zeus laugh, Dionysus hated that play, and I tended to agree with him. "You may as well ask him about it yourself."

Cameron blinked at me. "Ask who?"

"My nephew, of course… your step-son now, if you want to be technical. Your child will be his brother."

Cameron laughed thinly and rubbed his hands over his stomach protectively. "I keep forgetting," he said quietly. I regarded him carefully and wondered how much of the reality of this new world had really sunk into the young man's mind. That he had accepted Zeus and his own role in the rebuilding of Olympus was one thing; but when it came to family, there was quite a bit more to digest.

"You'll have a chance to meet them all soon, I have no doubt. Now that Zeus has proven that the prophecy is real, those who doubted will be returning to Olympus. No doubt Zeus will make a big deal of the arrival of his child." I turned away and walked down the aisle as I spoke.

"Why aren't they here already?" Cameron's voice followed me as he struggled to keep up.

"They have their reasons," I said with a dark chuckle. "We all still have work to do. Even if mankind has forgotten us, the seasons still turn, men still die..."

"I still don't understand what happened," he said.

"Neither do we," I replied stiffly. The lie stuck in my throat. We all knew the reason why Hera had plotted against us, but not all of us had accepted it the way Poseidon had. Hera's curse had been a personal vendetta, but the goddess was as hotheaded as her husband, and had tarnished us all. Poseidon had taken the whole mess more personally than he should have... but my own experience was much different.

It had been the beginning of Persephone's six-month stay in the Underworld. As always, she was sweet, caring, and always seeking to find ways to please me. She began in my library, dusting and organizing, and lamenting the state of some of her favorite tomes. She kept me company as I read—bringing me food and drink, trying to make me smile with songs and stories she had heard during her months spent in the summer sun.

"Hades," she had said, the lilt of her voice telling me that she was about to ask me for a favor that I might not be inclined to grant. "These books are in a dreadful state, and I worry that you have neglected them in my absence."

It was a preposterous notion; I should have known that something was amiss as soon as the words had left her crimson lips. But instead, I took the bait.

"Are you questioning my care of this library?" I asked as mildly as I knew how.

Persephone's tinkling laughter flitted towards me; sometimes I can still hear the sound of it in the depths of the library, so many centuries later. "Oh no, husband, I am merely suggesting that your lack of care is beginning to show… and on my favorite books too…"

I remembered how the tone of her voice had settled over me, and how it had infuriated me that she would even suggest such a thing. "What are you trying to say?"

Persephone had sniffed in her elegant way and plucked a book from the stack. She opened it with languid fingers and began to turn the pages. The leather binding creaked softly as her hand caressed it and I could only grind my teeth in frustration as she stayed silent, pretending to read the carefully inked words. "I am only your wife for six months of the year," she said thoughtfully.

"You are my wife all year," I said through clenched teeth.

"Is that so?" She said without meeting my eyes. "My sisters tell me that you spend a great deal of your time on earth, consorting with mortals…"

"Your sisters…"

"Yes," she interrupted me. "My sisters. Perhaps they chose rightly to remain unmarried. At least they will not be disappointed in their spouse…"

"You begin to sound like your mother more every day," was all I could say. "I do not need to prove my fidelity to you. Nor would I if you asked."

Persephone slowly tore a page from the book; the sound of the parchment fibers separating from the binding grated on my spine; hot anger burned in my chest as I watched her drop it unceremoniously to the stone floor. She took another page between her slender fingers and repeated her action. Tearing the page slowly from the ancient book, one that I recognized as a gift I had given her many years ago.

"No… you have always been absurdly secretive about your conquests. Not like your brothers," she said. Her voice was calm and she tore another page and dropped it onto the floor with the others.

"Now I wonder if you have been speaking with Hera," I said. I could hear the strident, angry, voice of my brother's wife in every word Persephone spoke. This was her argument, not my wife's. The candlelight glittered off the crown of golden wheat that adorned Persephone's brow. A crown she usually set aside when her time with me began. *How had I not noticed?*

"What if I have?" she asked. "What words did you last have to speak to the Queen of Heaven?"

I gritted my teeth and glared at my wife. I would never bow to Hera, and she knew it. *They all knew it.*

"She knows very well the last words I spoke to her," I said with a smile. I remembered them well… *"Get the hell out of my library, wench."*

"Perhaps you should have been more careful," she said, closing the book sharply.

"And what is *that* supposed to mean?"

"Hera's memory is long, and she is quicker to anger than she is to forget."

"Enough of this cryptic nonsense!" I roared. Persephone had the good sense to look frightened as the candles that flickered among the books flared brightly with my anger. The book she held slipped out of her hand and fell to the floor with the pages she had torn from its bindings. "Say what you mean or I will send you back to your mother, but I have a feeling that is what you want."

Persephone stood before me with defiant eyes, but her hands trembled ever so slightly as they plucked at her robes and smoothed her golden hair. "It has been too long that your brother has dishonored his Queen," she began, seeming to find some confidence in her own voice. But I could still hear Hera's bitterness behind it. What care did she have over the state of Zeus' marriage? We, all of us, knew how Hera raged behind closed doors at him. Her anger had been no secret.

There was a *crash* from the stairwell and I could hear Cerberus' sharp bark of surprise. "What is the meaning of this?" I said, my voice deadly quiet.

Persephone's steady, violet gaze never left mine, but then the smell of smoke hit my nostrils and the unease I'd felt suddenly blossomed into panic as the sound of crackling flames reached my ears.

My library.

With the faintest smile on her face, Persephone reached out and tipped a candle off the shelf and onto the floor. The flame licked at the dry pages she had dropped there and I stamped them out with a shocked cry. The flames crushed, I gripped my wife's arms and shook her. "What have you done?" I shouted in her face. But Persephone didn't even flinch, though I must have hurt her with the strength of my grip.

Without another word, I threw her aside and raced into the stacks, searching for the source of the blaze I knew was raging through my precious books.

Cerberus' howling echoed in the halls as I ran, and I could hear my wife's tinkling laughter and the *slap* of her golden sandals on the marble steps that led back up to Olympus.

Betrayed.

I pulled my cloak from my shoulders, prepared to smother the blaze, but then the heat hit me like a wall, knocking me off balance. I crashed into a stack of books, spilling them over the floor. The fire roared in my ears as it devoured my precious books.

I threw my cloak over the nearest pile and did what I could to try to beat the flames back, but my efforts were futile and the fire raged around me. I shouted and cursed and tried everything I could think of, but the fire was enchanted by my wife's magic, and nothing I did would deter it.

"Uncle!" A shout from behind made me turn. My nephew Hermes' blond head bobbed between the aisles as he ran through the shelves towards me. I sighed with relief at seeing him, because with him came a cold gale that blew through the library. The flames, emboldened by Persephone's magic, battled against the wind briefly, seeming to grow momentarily. But, Hermes' gray eyes narrowed as he reached my side and I could feel the focus of his godly powers as the winds howled through the dark chamber and narrow corridors.

My nephew's expression changed as the fire resisted his power, and I braced myself against the stone wall as I felt the wind begin to shift. "Persephone is behind this!" I roared.

Books and papers flew through the air as Hermes focused his winds on the flames, finally beating them back and scattering the embers over the stone floor.

My nephew leaned against a charred bookshelf, panting lightly as he surveyed the damage. "What did you do now?" he asked with a half-smile.

I glared at him and at the ruin of my library.

Centuries of collecting—'hoarding' she had called it—ruined in an instant. Persephone had never been cruel like this, but her mother had never forgiven me and I wondered who she had been listening to in her time away from my side.

"That was a trick question, uncle. You do enough just being yourself," Hermes said. He set his hands upon his hips and kicked one of the blackened books that lay at my feet. "My father is looking for you."

"Is he?" I threw a scorched book against the wall in a fit of anger. "He can fucking *wait*."

"I don't think he will."

"Too bad for him."

Hermes was silent, and the minutes stretched between us. "What?" I roared.

"Hera is here," he said simply.

"Why should I care about that?"

Hermes shrugged. "I'm just the messenger," he said, and then he was gone.

"Uhh..."

Cameron's unsteady voice jolted me out of the past and back to my library. I ran my hand along the bookshelf—un-burnt—the library rebuilt. Centuries had passed, but my anger hadn't faded, and I could still smell the smoke from that fire.

"What?" My voice was deadly quiet and Cameron cleared his throat.

"Nothing... I was just wondering if you were going to tell me—"

"Tell you what?" My eyes burned into his, and Cameron took a wary step back. "Tell you what happened? Tell you how Persephone and the other goddesses distracted us so that they could lay their curse upon us without our knowledge? Did you want to hear me say that it was my fault? Did Zeus send you down here for that?"

Cameron's eyes were wide as he stared at me, but I didn't care if I was frightening him. Rage boiled through my veins like lava and there was nowhere for me to direct my anger but at the young man who trembled in front of me. I couldn't harm him, of course, but those mortal habits were hard to shake off.

I had blamed myself for so many centuries. If I had ignored Persephone, if I had not taken the time to argue with her, perhaps I would have known that Hera was up to no good. But after the fire, after Hermes had come to fetch me, I had sat across from the Queen of Heaven while we dined; I drank the wine Persephone poured for me and listened to Athena's stories as my brothers smiled their approval.

I gritted my teeth and tightened my grip on the bookshelf. The dark wood cracked beneath my fingers and I glared down at Cameron. "Well?" I shouted.

Cameron yelped a little and took another step back. "N-no," he stammered. "I just wanted to find out what happened."

"Curiosity killed the cat," I said darkly. Cameron swallowed thickly and plucked a book from the shelf near his head.

"I can see you're busy…"

"Very." I looked at the book in his hand meaningfully. "Herodotus? Good luck with that. I expect to see it back on the shelf as soon as you're done with it. Or as soon as you give up."

Cameron laughed awkwardly and backed away down the aisle before he turned and ran, a little unsteadily, away from me.

I allowed myself a small smile. *Petty victories.* My brothers could celebrate their prizes as they saw fit, but I saw no need to flaunt anything. They might believe that they had beaten Hera's curse… but at what cost? Putting these mortals in danger, was it worth it? How cavalier, how arrogant were they to believe that they could protect their sparks from Hera's wrath. Poseidon had come close to losing Brooke, something he couldn't admit, not even in private, but I could see it in his eyes, and I could see the haunted look that hovered over Brooke. Even with his new cloak of immortality, the young man still held fear in his heart.

They could keep their prophecy. And they could stay away from me.

CHAPTER 2 ~ GIDEON

I'm pretty sure that when my mother suggested a 'change of scenery' for my post-graduate work she'd expected that I'd stay in Boston or even move back to Concord and into my childhood bedroom—not halfway around the world to Rome. I'd been fantasizing about moving overseas for as long as I could remember, but that's what growing up in a small town can do to you.

I leaned out the window above my bed and stared out over the Piazza Navona and the ancient city I now called home and took a deep breath. I loved the smell of this place. The sound of the church bells, the bustle of the streets, and the elusive sparkle of the Tiber... my apartment was almost certainly illegal. The money I paid to the man who lived downstairs definitely didn't reflect its quality. But for this view... I'd pay anything.

My apartment, if you could call it that, was dark and draughty, and a pair of pigeons had made a nest in the corner near the door. I didn't mind them so much, and it was nice to have company when I came home late from the library. Besides, it was close to work, and there was no way I was going to complain about that.

"You're an archivist, a history major... you can work anywhere! Why do you have to go so far away?"

It was as though I could hear my mother's voice echoing in my tiny excuse for an apartment. I'd only been in Rome for a year, and it seemed like every week I'd receive a letter from her full of hope that I wasn't enjoying myself and that I needed to come home.

"All you need to do is say the word and I'll have you back on a plane heading for the States... don't forget... just one word, Gideon."

I rested my chin on my arm and watched the sun rising over the city.

Why the hell would I want to go back to Boston?

My ancient travel clock buzzed on the windowsill next to me and I stopped it gently and re-set the alarm. This clock had been through a lot, had been repaired more times that I could count, and I honestly didn't know what I'd do with myself when it finally died. I reluctantly pulled myself away from the window and rolled off the bed.

As soon as my feet hit the floor, I heard a shout from the apartment below mine and I smiled just a little. *Without fail.*

"*Buongiorno, signor Tavatti,*" I said loudly.

A loud stream of muffled Italian cursing was the only reply I ever received for my efforts. I shook my head and grabbed my towel. The shared bathroom was on the same floor as the old man's apartment, and I could hear him cursing through the weathered door as I padded to the shower. My grasp of the language was getting better, and I'd learned all the swear words I'd ever need from him.

It was the same every morning. Up at dawn, listen to Mr. Tavatti shout at whatever was making noise, and then make my way to the library to take my place in the archives.

The *Biblioteca Vallicelliana* was almost hidden, easy to miss if you're not looking for it. The door was mundane enough—a wide wooden door painted black that looked like it had been there since the library opened its doors in 1644—barely out of place in this area of the city. Some days there were even cars parked across it that blocked the entrance to anyone but those who really wanted to find us.

This might not have been the position any average college grad would want. But I was twenty-six, and as my mother liked to remind me, I was a 'super nerd.' She wasn't wrong, and I wasn't about to hide from that fact. This was what I wanted. To be surrounded by history on the streets, and enveloped in it at my job. I wouldn't trade anything for the way these ancient rooms smelled, and the way I felt when I walked through that black door and stepped inside.

The library had always been my 'safe place.' When I was a kid, my mother always said that if I ever wandered off, she could always find me in the book aisle of the grocery store. Some kids went straight for the toys or the bulk food bins, but I went straight for the books and magazines. My friends at school always tried to reach for the foil wrapped magazines their fathers brought home, but I always had my nose in whatever book looked like it had the most pages. Sure, I'd read a few things I probably shouldn't have at a very young age, but books were my life, and I'm sure my mother appreciated the quiet my obsession afforded her.

While she was doing night school, I was doing homework way above my grade level and the librarians at the Boston Public Library all knew me by name. Now, I was apprenticed to one of the most respected archivists in Europe, if not the world, and I spent my days with the things I loved best in the whole world: *words*.

Some people came here to see the beautifully illuminated bible that had been owned by Charlemagne… but my favorite section in the *Vallicelliana* was the collection of books that had been banned by the Catholic Church. It was delightfully blasphemous to handle them in such a devout city, and I made a point of checking on them every day to be sure that everything was in its place.

The familiar creak of the floorboards beneath my feet and the cushioned silence of the library always brought a smile to my face, and I stood in the doorway with my eyes closed, just letting the stillness settle over me. After the bustle of the Piazza Navona, the stillness was pure bliss.

This was what I envisioned heaven would be like.

"Gideon!"

A shout echoed through the library, and I winced as a chorus of *shhh's* followed the cry. A new cadre of volunteers had been brought in for what our director, Dottore Mariano, called our 'busy season.' While we didn't see a huge rise in foot traffic at this time of year, it was enough that he had decided to put up notices at the local hostels and backpacker's inns to catch anyone who might be interested in acting as a street atlas for lost wanderers, or point actual patrons to their proper sections of the library.

I opened my eyes carefully, hoping that the shout had been a false alarm.

"Gideon! Up here!"

Nope.

With gritted teeth I ignored the stares of those reading between the stacks and walked into the *Sala Monumentale* across the hall from the main reception desk. The high-ceilinged room was lined with two-story stacks of precious leather-bound books and I walked across the threshold with my sternest librarian expression plastered on my face.

On the second floor of the vast room was Emilie, one of the newer volunteers. She had just arrived from London, and claimed to be working on her applications for a Masters Program and a classical literature post in Exeter, respectively. If that was really her intention, I hadn't seen any sign of it. She leaned over the balcony and wiggled her fingers at me.

"Hey, hey, hey! I need you to do me a favor," she said loudly. Someone harrumphed loudly in the corner. I glared up at her and pointed to the hidden spiral staircase in the corner that led to the second floor. "Oh, fine, fine," she huffed and disappeared from the railing.

I flinched at the sound of her boots on the spiral stairs and at the loud creak of the wooden floorboards as she jumped down the final stairs.

"So, yeah, I'm glad you're here—" she began. I pressed my lips together and grabbed her arm. I dragged her, protesting, towards the front desk. An elderly gentleman fixed us with a glare of admonishment, and I tightened my grip on Emilie's arm.

She yelped quietly and picked up her pace to keep up with me.

When we reached the desk I let her go and crossed my arms across my chest.

"What?" I asked through gritted teeth.

Emilie rubbed her arm and then batted her eyelashes at me, instantly recovered. "You're *just* the person I wanted to see today, Gideon," she purred.

I raised an eyebrow. That could only mean one thing. "Look, Em, I have a busy day ahead of me. I don't have time to—"

"It won't take all day, I promise!" She interrupted me by grabbing my hands and tugging on them sharply. "I just have a quick appointment and then I'll be back! Signore de Sarno won't even notice you're not in the archive room. I *promise*. You're just the sweetest, and you're doing me the *biggest* favor… pleeeease?" She blinked up at me and pushed out her bottom lip in an exaggerated pout.

Did that actually work on anyone… ever?

"I'll owe you bigtime. I'll bring you back gelato from that place you love!"

"Em, it's ten in the morning…"

"Exactly! Gelato for breakfast, *Viva Italia*! You're the best, thank you so much!"

Before I could argue or even close my mouth, Emilie had grabbed her backpack from behind the desk and planted a kiss on my cheek before she ran out the door.

"Uhhh…"

"Shhh!" Came the reply from an angry looking older gentleman hunched over one of the map tables.

I smothered my groan of annoyance and took my place behind the desk. With any luck, it would be a quiet morning; but my luck had never been very good, or particularly useful, and today wasn't shaping up any differently.

"Bloody volunteers," I muttered as I refilled the tourist maps and straightened literally everything in the reception area. Emilie was one of three volunteers who had come on in the last month. She wasn't the best we'd had, but she was the most reliable, and her Italian wasn't as horrible as some of our volunteers' had been. With a long sigh, I put on my best customer service face and tried to prepare myself for the day.

This 'favor' I'd been roped into would set me back in my work more than I liked, but now that I was here, I could appreciate the library a little more.

Being in the archive rooms wasn't the worst thing, but once I settled into my temporary post, I remembered how much I liked being a part of the living, breathing, life of the library and how much I enjoyed the people who came every day to pay their respects to hundreds of years of knowledge and learning.

I wasn't even ashamed to admit that I was hoping to see one patron in particular… in the year I'd been at the library I had never really met the man, and we'd only exchanged a few words in passing. Behind his imposing glare and his gruff, heavily accented replies I could sense that there was something different about him. As though he didn't quite belong. He wasn't the youngest patron of the *Vallicelliana*, but his appetite for books was well known among the senior staff and Dottore Mariano had allowed him to examine some very fragile and valuable works with perfect trust.

This particular gentleman always had strange requests for the volunteers, and I'd seen more than one turn away from him with a hunted expression and shaking hands, as though they'd received a threat upon their lives and not a query about a book or piece of archival material.

I knew all of our 'regulars,' but not him. And for some reason, that intrigued me. It didn't help that I have a well-documented (thanks, Facebook) weakness for tall, tattooed nerds. Trapped in the archive room, there was little chance that we'd ever speak, and it was probably for the best.

I had terrible taste in men.

I greeted the regulars as they arrived and helped them with their selections; and when the day began to warm, I drew maps and gave directions to sweating tourists who wanted nothing more than a cold drink but were walking in circles in the Piazza instead.

"Gideon! Oh, my god, I was gone soooo much longer than I expected. I'm soooo sorry!"

I looked up from the map I was drawing as Emilie bounded up the stairs. Her long black braid bounced against her shoulder and she swept it away with an impatient and dramatic sigh.

The tourist I was helping fired a glance filled with annoyance in her direction and I fixed Emilie with a glare of my own and focused my attention back on the map.

Not taking any kind of a hint, Emilie pushed her way through the crowd and flopped down into the wooden chair behind the desk. It creaked in protest as she rocked absently. The old springs whined at the unfamiliar motion and I winced. "You would not *believe* the crowds today," she groaned loudly. "Tourists *everywhere*. There must be a cruise ship at Civitavecchia for the weekend."

I finished my map and watched the grumbling tour group make its way down the stairs and out into the street before turning to face her. The chair was too close and I felt trapped between her and the heavy wooden desk. She smiled as she looked up at me through dark lashes. *What was her deal?*

"There are *three* cruise ships at Civitavecchia right now," I said quietly, "and it feels like most of their passengers have been here today."

"Oooo, lucky you," she said as she rocked on the chair again.

I pointed at the clock meaningfully, and her gaze followed my finger slowly. "You've been gone for *hours*, and Signore de Sarno is going to turn my hide into bookbinding leather!" I narrowed my eyes at her. "What were you doing, anyway?"

She looked far too happy to have been at any kind of 'appointment.'

"Oh! Nothing much… I met this guy—Nicos, or maybe Marco, I

can't remember, but he promised to buy me the best espresso in Rome, but—"

"You made me sit here all morning while you went on an *espresso date* with some guy you just met?" My voice was quiet, but my frustration should have been clear in my tone.

Emilie blinked at me; her pale eyes held an expression of confusion that I'd grown used to seeing there. I groaned and leaned against the desk.

"It wasn't *really* a date, I mean I guess it would have been but—"

"Shut up, Em," I cut her off with a wave of my hand. "Just shut up. Next time, call in sick. And don't ever ask me for another favor." I glared at her again. "And let me guess… No gelato?"

Emilie opened her empty hands and looked guilty for just a moment. "No?" she said in a small voice. "I'll make it up to you, I promise!" she cried. Before I could move, she had scooted the chair farther forward and wrapped her arms around my waist so she could hug me tightly.

"Oh, noooo… No, no. I have to go." I pried her arms off my hips, trying to ignore the way they lingered and tried to slide lower.

*Did the girl have no self-awareness **and** no gay-dar?*

"Rain check!" she called after me as I pulled my bag over my shoulder and fled down the hallway towards the archive room.

My face was probably red, and I kept my eyes on the toes of my Converse as I walked delicately over the hardwood floors, careful to avoid the spots that creaked the loudest.

I was almost at the door when something crashed against my shoulder, spinning me into the wall.

"Ow! What the fuck? Watch it!" I said aloud before immediately feeling stupid. The narrow hallway was empty.

"What the hell?" I whispered. I thought I heard a chuckle, and my heart beat just a little faster, but then one of the sparrows that somehow always found their way into the library flew from its hidden perch towards the front desk. I shook my head. "Now you're hearing things," I muttered.

"And you're talking to yourself…"

I yelped in surprise as the face of my mentor appeared in the doorway of the archive room. Signore de Sarno was a pleasantly dusty gentleman whose hair was always in some manner of disarray and who always smelt of a mixture of expensive tobacco, ink, and leather polish.

"Signore," I stammered, "*Mi dispiace sono in ritardo…* I was helping one of the volunteers…"

"Ah, Emilie," he said sagely. "She caught Vittorio the same way last week. Let me guess… a mysterious appointment?"

I nodded, feeling like a moron.

"Ah, yes," he said with a smile. "No matter now, Gideon, come along."

I nodded and ducked under his arm and into the sanctuary of the archive room. I groaned inwardly when I saw the stack of books that had been placed on my desk. It was going to be a long day.

CHAPTER 3 ~ HADES

I had borne many things in the centuries since my birth. The indignity of bowing to my youngest brother had chafed the most, until the day I'd discovered the role that my own wife had played in the curse Hera had laid upon Olympus.

Being banished to the Underworld was nothing to this betrayal. *I should have known. I should have suspected that the Queen of Heaven would attempt to twist Persephone against me. Demeter had probably given her the idea. If it hadn't been for that damned fire... If she hadn't distracted me, maybe I could have stopped it.*

I slammed my fist against the marble wall and watched flakes of mortar float to the stone floor to mix with the dust at my feet. This was an argument I'd had with myself time and time again... and every time the ending was the same. What could I have done?

Nothing.

By the time Hermes had come and blown away Persephone's enchanted flames, Hera had already done her work, and we sat there in blissful ignorance as the goddess's curse settled over us.

I still remember the look on Hera's face... there was something faintly satisfied and smug about her expression—more so than usual. It took some time for the curse to take effect, but as with so many things, Zeus was the first of us to discover what had happened.

He had returned to Olympus, his eyes red and his face streaked with salt tears as he described the beautiful girl who had died screaming in his arms while his divine seed burned her from the inside out. At first we did not believe him. It seemed too horrible to imagine. To reveal ourselves in our truly divine form was death to mortals, that much we knew, and Zeus had learned that lesson centuries earlier.

Spurred by Hera's whispers, a princess of Thebes whom Zeus had taken as a lover, had demanded that her lover reveal his true identity. So unrelenting was she in her pleading that Zeus finally complied... Semele was the first casualty of Hera's jealousy; her death forced Zeus, King of the Gods, to nurture her unborn child from his own flesh—my nephew Dionysus. But Semele had been directly influenced by the goddess. *This was different.*

And there would be more.

One, by one, each of the gods reported similar tales of horror. How their lovers, men and women in the prime of life, died in pain and misery while they were powerless to help or heal them. The memory of each of those deaths weighed heavily upon my brothers and nephews for countless centuries.

For some, the wounds were still too fresh, and to see Zeus now... I wondered how his joy affected those Olympians who had not accepted what had happened, or those who could not let go of the past.

Cameron was the physical embodiment of the prophecy made real, and Zeus could not have acted like more of a fool because of it. His pride had always been legendary, but that was eclipsed by this victory over Hera. With every passing day, Cameron seemed to grow more beautiful, and Zeus made sure that anyone within earshot knew about it. The young man was growing into his divinity, and his pregnancy, and it was clear to everyone which goddess had contributed to his divine heritage.

I watched from the shadows as Zeus coddled and cajoled his lover with every delicacy he could find. Any precious thing that Cameron requested he brought with no complaints and I catalogued them all.

I had never seen my brother like this. Any of my nephews could attest to the fact that Zeus was a notoriously absent father, and I wondered if some of that bitterness was what kept Ares and the others away from Olympus so long. Now that the prophecy had been proven real, Zeus had sent Hermes on a mission to locate every one of the Olympians and tell them that Hera's curse could be defeated.

Rebuilding Olympus had seemed like a foolish dream, the lonely plans of an impotent deity... but now things could progress in earnest and Zeus was eager for the birth of his child.

I gritted my teeth as I suddenly regretted shouting at Cameron. He was a kind young man—better than my brother deserved, surely. And I was certain that it would not take long for my hot-headed brother to come stomping down the stairs to my library to scold me for treating him unfairly.

Poseidon was dealing with his own mortal... With the discovery of his own spark, my waterlogged brother had transformed from a wet fish to a passionate defender of Zeus' claims. I expected he would bring his own lover back to Olympus very soon. But even sooner than that, there would be the squalling of newborn babes echoing off the marble columns of Olympus—a sound that none of us had heard in centuries.

While Zeus hungered for the moment he would hold his child in his arms, I could think of a thousand things I would rather do. *More than a thousand.*

Zeus' triumph was in defeating his wife. Yes, he would rebuild Olympus with divine occupants who would love and adore him, but he had merely avoided the curse. It had not been lifted. Now that he had found Cameron it seemed he had forgotten what kind of danger our attentions brought into the lives of the mortals who had been chosen for us.

Brooke, Poseidon's mortal, had almost died—and the daughters of Nereus had been eager to do Hera's bidding. What else was lurking in the shadows? Zeus' thoughts may have been consumed with Cameron and the birth of his child… but what of the rest of us? My selfish brother, never looking beyond his own desires. If Hera's curse did not linger, there would be nothing to stop him from returning to his old ways.

Persephone had often tried to change me… and every attempt had failed. But this curse, it had changed all of us for eternity.

"You finally succeeded," I muttered darkly.

"At what? I can't recall a time that I've failed, brother… are you talking to yourself again?"

Almost instinctively, the hand that rested against the wall curled into a fist and I straightened as Zeus bounded down the stairs and into my library.

"Do you see any better company?" I growled.

Zeus waggled a finger in my direction and I frowned. I hated him when he was like this, and he was always like this lately. "Now, Hades, you should not be here in your dull library." He poked at a stack of books that tilted precariously towards me. I reached out to steady them with a firm hand. "You should be down on earth searching for your spark. I know there is one out there for each of us!"

"That may be," I said dryly. "But if I had known you had planned to turn Olympus into a nursery so quickly, I would have translated that prophecy differently."

Zeus laughed and clapped me on the back and I gritted my teeth. "Well, you can't put a timer on divine seed, brother. If the Fates want Olympus rebuilt, who am I to stand in their way?"

"The Fates haven't spoken to us in centuries," I said.

"Yes… well. A figure of speech. Old habits die hard." Zeus paused for a moment and regarded me with an arched eyebrow. "Speaking of old habits… I'll thank you to speak more kindly to Cameron in the future. He merely wanted—"

"To waste my time and mis-file my books," I interrupted him briskly and pushed his hand off my shoulder. I was never in the mood for brotherly affection, and the air around Olympus had put me more on edge than I liked to admit.

"Be that as it may, I want him as happy, content, and healthy as possible before the birth of our son, and I won't have you complicating things. Or ruining everything I have planned."

"Healthy? He's one of us now, he will always be *healthy*..." Was there even such a thing as an unhealthy god? An unhealthy appetite was one thing, and we'd already been punished for that.

"It's just an expression!" Zeus shouted. His gray eyes shone silver in the dim light of the library and I allowed myself a dark chuckle. I loved pushing my brother's buttons. He was just so... easy. So predictable. That was how Hera had done it, after all. If there was anything the King of the Gods could be relied upon for, it was his predictability.

Zeus raked a hand through his hair and let out a gusty sigh before leaning against one of the bookshelves. It creaked under his weight and I glared at my brother, but as usual, he didn't seem to notice. "You have to be here for the birth... you know that, right?"

I nodded sternly and crossed my arms over my chest, my eyes on the creaking bookshelf. "Hermes told me."

"Well, now I'm telling you myself so you can't pretend that you didn't get the message. I expect you to be there. Cameron expects you to be there."

I raised an eyebrow. "Does the mortal know we're all going to be watching?"

Zeus had the grace to look a little flustered. "No. No... of course not. You won't be *watching*, you'll just be there. With the others."

"The others."

My brother was getting more flustered with every passing second, and I was enjoying his discomfort immensely. "Yes... the others! This is the sign everyone is waiting for. The birth of a healthy child—my son—will be the moment that changes their minds about the prophecy."

I rolled my eyes at his earnestness and plucked a book from the top of a nearby pile. "Have you chosen a name?"

"A name?"

"The newest member of the pantheon needs a name, does he not? And are you so sure it will be a boy?" I opened the book and looked at my brother carefully. He squirmed under my gaze and I tried not to smile.

"I promised Cameron that he could choose the name," Zeus mumbled.

"Oh, lovely," I sneered. "And what names are popular on earth right now? All hail, Skylar... God of Summer Winds." I gestured grandly. "Or perhaps, Zoe... Goddess of those obnoxious spring storms you're so fond of..."

"Careful, brother," Zeus' voice was deadly quiet, and I allowed myself to smile.

"Perhaps you should choose the child's name," I said with a wink and turned another page in my book.

"When it is your turn to fall in love, I shall take great pleasure in making jokes at your expense."

I snorted in reply.

"You scoff at me now," Zeus said. "But you wait. Your time will come."

"You make it sound like a curse," I spat. "I have had my fill of curses."

My brother yawned and stepped away from the bookshelf. "Enough of this," he said. "Has anyone ever told you how tiresome your constant glowering and growling can be, brother?"

I looked up at him, my eyes blazing. "Only my wife," I said through gritted teeth.

Zeus smirked at me and walked away through the bookshelves and stacks of dusty books. "You should really get someone to clean down here... you should find yourself a mortal who loves you enough to do the work."

"Get out!" I roared.

Zeus' laughter floated back to me down the marble stairs and I flung the book I had been pretending to read across the room.

What right did he have to lecture me? He had found his 'spark.' And Poseidon... he was close to bringing his spark back to Olympus permanently. But how long would it be for the rest of us? Hermes, as always, seemed to be in no rush to do anything but his duty. Ares had been absent for more time than Zeus would want to admit, that was sure. Apollo had said nothing... and while he had agreed to oversee the birth of the newest Olympian, even I didn't know where he stood, or what his plans were. The true test of the prophecy would be in the birth. Cameron would be tested—more than any mortal had ever been tested. This child was our future.

Future. It seemed a ridiculous notion for an immortal being to ponder, yet, against my will, I was pondering it.

It didn't take long for Poseidon to return to Olympus with his own mortal in tow. I should have known by the determined set of my brother's brow that trouble was brewing. If I'd cared enough, I could have watched him from the marble cistern... but I had more pressing matters to attend to.

Like Zeus, Poseidon's mortal was sweet and biddable. But the God of the Seas had been gifted with a mortal who was as shy and reserved as the goddess who had contributed to his origin. Cameron was quick to form a bond with this new addition to Olympus. Brooke seemed fascinated by the swell of Cameron's stomach, and I watched from the shadows as his eyes widened as he felt the child kick.

"Have you ever seen anything so beautiful?"

"Many things," I grumbled as Poseidon strode through the marble columns towards me. Cameron and Brooke walked away from us, their heads bent together while they talked quietly, still oblivious to our presence. "What now, brother? Will you waste no time in setting a child in your spark's belly?"

Poseidon shook his head. "I am not in the same hurry as our brother. Brooke is different... and he will need time to adjust."

I leaned against the column and crossed my arms over my chest. "So, have you come to chide me as well?" I asked with an arched brow.

"Zeus will be in earnest now, that much is true. But I have not come here to lecture you... I came to tell you that you were right."

I felt a smile creep across my face. "I don't need your validation, brother."

"Perhaps not, but all the same—" Poseidon paused for just a moment before meeting my eyes. "I thought you were lying. Not about the prophecy, every time I touch Brooke I can feel for myself that it's true."

"But?"

"But the danger we put them in... the goddesses knew that I had found him. Somehow, I'd marked him."

I frowned just a little at my brother's distress; he looked almost guilty.

"I don't know how to explain it, but something about our touch—our intimacy—it reveals them to the goddesses. Hera sent the daughters of Nereus after Brooke." My brother's voice grew quiet and his unwavering gaze held mine. "They almost killed him."

"And what did you do to them?" I asked. I wasn't sure I knew what I would do if faced with the same predicament, but revenge was something I was very good at, and Hera knew that.

Poseidon waved off my question. "It doesn't matter. What matters is that Brooke is safe. Hera is growing bolder... we have to be sure that we are prepared—"

"Prepared? For what? To defend ourselves?"

Poseidon shook his head. "To protect our mortals. When you find your spark, you have to be sure that they will accept you, that they will accept everything being offered. If they don't, if they don't believe you, or any of us, we won't be able to protect them from Hera's rage."

"You had better tell your tales to the others, brother," I scoffed. "It does me little good."

There was a hint of derision in my brother's gaze now. "You believe you're immune to all of this, don't you? Is the Lord of the Underworld above something as petty as love?"

"Bah."

"I see," Poseidon replied. "Our brother, Zeus, used to believe he was above all of these mortal concerns... but look at him now. About to become a father. You've seen him with Cameron. I have to admit, I barely recognize him."

"How Hera would laugh if she could see this," I said with a sneer. "That her curse would have entirely the opposite effect than intended. This is the Zeus she always wanted, is it not? Attentive and loving, gentle and constant… all it took was a little curse." I laughed grimly and Poseidon glared at me.

"Don't let him hear you say that," he said quietly.

"Or what? What will my mighty brother do to me? Nothing. He will be too afraid to wake the children," I sneered.

"Fine. Keep your snarling and growling in your library where they belong. If you want no part of this, that is your choice… but remember what I said, brother."

The marble chamber echoed with my laughter as I willed myself to earth and left my brother standing alone in the colonnade.

He could keep his condescending speeches about love and forgiveness; they both could. Let them wander the halls of Olympus with a herd of children. As long as they stayed out of my library and didn't touch my dog… I could learn to live with the noise, but there was no way I would be contributing to it. *I had better things to do.*

CHAPTER 4 ~ GIDEON

I tried my best to steer clear of Emilie for the rest of the week, but the girl had a knack for knowing where I'd be... All I wanted to do was my job, but she was making that a little awkward.

"Gideooonnnn... just the handsome lad I've been waiting for all my life," she purred in my ear one day while I was restocking the shelves on the second floor of the library. When I'd first come up here, I'd been elated to see that the stacks were deserted, but now I wished for some company (that wasn't her) more than anything.

"I've been hiding in the library," I said with a weak laugh and squirmed away from the fingers that kneaded my shoulders with just a little too much familiarity than I was comfortable with. Emilie had only been volunteering with us for a short time, and while I didn't want to be rude... this was also really uncomfortable.

"Do people tell you that you're funny?" She asked with a sly smile. All I could do was shrug in reply.

"Not really."

"Soooo, Gid... I have to ask you something—"

"No. No, no, no," I said firmly. "No more favors. That last little stunt you pulled put me behind in my work by about three days."

Emilie sulked prettily and I rolled my eyes.

"Ugh. Don't remind me. He never even called," she said sadly, but she brightened in an instant as something seemed to occur to her. "I have an idea… why don't we take off for the afternoon. You're a nerd; you probably know the best museum in the city. Take me there!"

I stared at her incredulously. "I'm not a volunteer, I can't just 'take off' and go wandering around the city whenever I feel like it. I have a job. Responsibilities." I narrowed my eyes at her meaningfully. "Have you even *had* a job before?" That last part probably wasn't necessary, but I needed her to leave me the hell alone so I could finish re-cataloging the books on the trolley in front of me. *Who the hell did she think she was, ordering me around like that?*

Emilie leaned on the trolley and trailed her fingers over the cover of the nearest book. I resisted the urge to slap her hand away as she moved to pick it up.

"Don't you have something to do?" I snapped. I pulled the book out of her fingers and set it onto the shelf.

"Don't be like that, Gideon, I was just trying to have a little fun. You seem so… uptight."

"It's none of your business what I am," I said shortly. This 'cute' little game she was playing wasn't cute, and I was definitely not in the mood to humor her. All of a sudden, something dawned on me. "Emilie, you're the only volunteer here today… who's at the desk?"

Emilie blinked at me vacantly. "Um… no one, obviously. I'm right here."

"You're supposed to be at that desk for a reason! You have to sign in patrons and make sure no one walks out with one of the books…" I picked one up and waved it in her face. "These things are priceless!"

Emilie's eyes widened, as much at my unexpectedly angry tone as at the realization that her attempt at flirting could have much larger consequences.

"Why are you still here? Get the fuck downstairs and get behind that desk! If anything is missing or out of place… I swear to—"

A loud harrumph interrupted my tirade and I looked up—way up —into a pair of pale eyes that burned into mine like ice.

"*Posso aiutarti?* C-can I help you?" I stammered. My heart hammered in my throat as I took him in. He was tall. Taller than anyone I'd ever met, that was for sure. His hair was scraped back into a neat bun and his beard was trimmed. He was powerfully built, with broad shoulders and muscles that strained against the tailored shirt he wore. My eyes trailed down to his forearms, exposed by his rolled up shirtsleeves. They were covered in tattoos and scars, and I swallowed thickly as I tried desperately to make eye contact again while my stomach churned.

"I need to see Signore de Sarno," he said simply as he examined his nails. His expression was bored, and I cursed myself inwardly for being so awkward.

Emilie's eyes were wide, and I pushed her towards the spiral staircase that led down to the main floor. "I don't know where he is..." Emilie said quietly.

I gritted my teeth. "I'll go and find him, you need to get your ass back to that desk. I didn't even see him come up the stairs, he probably isn't even signed in," I hissed at her. Emilie scurried away without another word and I turned back to the huge, tattooed man with a lump in my throat. "Can I tell him who is here to see him?"

"I have an appointment," the man replied. His eyes met mine again and I felt a chill ripple down my spine. All I could do was nod.

"Right. Uh... I'll send him right up."

"Run along now," he said smoothly as he picked up one of the books on my trolley. I paused for a moment, watching him as he turned the pages carefully before setting it on the shelf.

"You shouldn't be doing that," I said before I could stop myself.

The man turned around and fixed me with that cold stare of his, and I felt my mouth go dry and the lump in my throat turn to concrete. "Oh, really. And are you going to stop me, librarian?"

"How did you get up here anyway? I didn't hear you come up the stairs, and I know I was alone up here—"

"Has anyone told you that you're far too talkative for a librarian?"

"All the time," I replied. The man didn't return my smile; he simply stared at me and then plucked another book from the trolley and examined the cover.

Silence settled between us, broken only by the creak of the floorboards from the room below. I shifted uncomfortably, knowing that I should fetch Signore de Sarno but not wanting to leave my books with this strange man who didn't look as though he belonged here at all. I'd seen him before; at least, I thought I had. But I couldn't be sure. I'd never been able to examine him closely before.

I opened my mouth to ask another question, but the man's cold gaze stopped me again and my stomach twisted tightly. There was a loud creak as someone climbed the spiral staircase, and I turned to see Signore de Sarno's wild white hair as he approached. I breathed a small sigh of relief, and felt some of the tightness in my belly begin to uncoil.

"Ah, my friend," my mentor said with a smile. "*Spero tu non abbia aspettato a lungo...*" He looked at me meaningfully and I nodded at him, suddenly feeling guilty for not rushing to the archive room to fetch him when I'd been asked.

The man smiled, and I could tell it wasn't something he did often, for the expression did little to warm the almost sinister nature of his features. The knot in my stomach tightened just a bit more as I watched Signore de Sarno lead him away to one of the hidden reading rooms that held some of our most precious collections.

Released from my obligation, I took my place at the trolley once more and began to shelve the newly repaired and catalogued books in their rightful places. I ran my hand along the spine of the book the man had held only a moment ago, and I could have sworn that it felt cold under my palm.

I was consumed with curiosity. I needed to know who the man was… and why I couldn't stop thinking about the way his muscles moved under his tattooed skin, and the way his cold eyes pierced through me. My chest felt hot and tight and I was sure that my neck was red by the time I finished re-filing my books and pulled my trolley back towards the ancient elevator.

I passed the room where Signore de Sarno had taken the man; I paused long enough to lean my ear against the door to listen to the man's deep voice rumble through the heavy wood. I couldn't hear what he was saying, but just the sensation of it gave me goosebumps and caused my breath to catch in my throat. I must have lingered too long, because the man stopped speaking abruptly and heavy footsteps came towards the door.

I pushed the cart frantically away, almost running towards the open elevator door. I flung the cart inside and slid the gate closed. Just as I threw the switch that started the elevator's motors, I looked up to see the tall man glowering at me, his arms crossed over his muscular chest. I felt my cheeks flaming as the elevator began to move, and I gasped as my stomach tightened again. The elevator slid below the floor and I was saved from the intensity of the man's gaze; but if the way my heart was pounding in my throat was any indication, I was in deep trouble.

Signore de Sarno didn't come back to the archive room, and I felt somewhat guilty to be locking up our office without saying goodnight. I sent the volunteer home and did a final check of the vast library to make sure that no one was hidden in the stacks or had fallen asleep on one of the map tables. It had happened before, which was why I'd insisted on being the last one out every night so I could double check.

I crept through the deserted main floor, turning off reading lamps and being careful not to make too much noise. If Signore de Sarno and the tall stranger were still in the reading room, I would leave them to whatever business they might have. But if not...

If not, what? Would you try and talk to him again like a complete ass? Maybe scold him for touching the books again?

I rubbed a hand against my forehead, reset my glasses on my nose, and stifled a groan. I was horrible at this stuff. I couldn't even remember the last time I'd been on a date. College maybe? I climbed the spiral staircase slowly, listening closely for any sound of voices, but the mezzanine was quiet.

As I placed my foot carefully on the top stair, I heard the door of the reading room open and the deep voice of the tall stranger as he spoke to Signore de Sarno.

"... I'll return as soon as it is ready and we can speak again about the manuscript. I believe it will be an excellent addition to the collection."

"*Un momento molto eccitante*," Signore de Sarno said hurriedly. "Gideon will be thrilled."

I would?

"Indeed," the man replied and I wondered what he meant. And what they were talking about. "*Buona notte*, Signore," he continued, "I will be seeing you again soon."

"Yes, of course."

My mentor's footsteps moved towards the staircase at the far side of the room, and I ducked behind a bookshelf to watch him. *But where was the stranger?* There was no other way out of the mezzanine except the elevator, and I would have heard it by now... I peered into the room, but all I could see were the shadows thrown by the soft golden glow of a lone reading lamp. I switched it off and stood still for just a moment.

I could hear Signore de Sarno moving around on the main floor, but that was it. And then I heard something... like a sharp intake of breath. A cold draft blew across the back of my neck; it sent goose-bumps shuddering down my spine and made me jump just a little.

"There shouldn't be any drafts up here," I muttered and rubbed my arms.

The sharp sound of the archive room door knocked me out of my curious trance and I ran for the staircase and down to the main floor. "Signore! Signore, don't lock me in!" I cried into the dark.

I looked back up at the mezzanine; feeling like someone was watching me. But there was nothing but darkness.

"Gideon! Come now, what are you still doing here? *Sbrigati!*"

"I'm coming," I said quietly. The silence of the library was comforting, but I was still unable to shake the feeling of being watched. I picked up my bag from where I'd dropped it and met Signore de Sarno at the front doors.

He smiled indulgently at me as I punched in the security code and took one last look at the mezzanine. Out of the corner of my eye, I thought I saw a shadow move in the darkness… but that was impossible.

"Is everything all right, Gideon?" Signore de Sarno asked.

"Yes… I think so. I just… it's been a long day."

Signore de Sarno nodded sagely and gestured at the black door that led out into the street. "Then it is high time you went home. We have a lot of work ahead of us."

"Of course, Signore. Good night."

It didn't matter how hard I tried, I couldn't seem to stop thinking about the tall man in the library—who was he? Why was he talking to Signore de Sarno so late into the night? And about what?

Curiosity killed the cat…

I poured some cheap wine into a cracked mug and tried to think about something else, anything but him. Anything but the way his long fingers caressed the leather bindings of the ancient books. Anything but the shiver that rushed up my spine at the thought of his cold eyes. Anything but the way my stomach twisted when he called me 'librarian' with a tone of dark disdain and sardonic humor in his voice. *What I wouldn't give to hear him say my name.*

I chuckled at myself and pulled my glasses off so I could rub my eyes. I'd been staring at books for too long. I drained my wine, climbed into bed, and stared out over the lights of Rome.

"Why would I ever go back to Boston?" I murmured aloud.

. . .

I was alone in the library, and it was dark, except for the glow of one of the reading lamps. "Why are you on?" I asked the shadows.

"I left it on," the voice came from the darkness and rolled over me like smoke. The words shuddered down my spine and my heart began to beat faster.

"Who are you?" I asked. My question was louder than I'd intended, and I was ashamed of the tremor in my voice. I cleared my throat and asked again, steadier this time. "Who are you? Come out of the shadows."

"Can you see me, librarian?"

That title again... my stomach twisted. "Yes," I whispered. I could see him, dark and threatening as he leaned against the bookshelf.

"You can only see me because I want you to," he said. "Tell me, librarian, do you like being watched?"

I swallowed thickly. "It's my job to watch the patrons of the library," I said as boldly as I dared.

"Ah, yes, of course," he said, and I could hear the ghost of a smile in his voice. "To keep them from snatching pages from your carefully curated collection. Of course. Books banned by the Catholic Church, holy relics and bibles that are centuries old... you worship them, do you not?"

"How can you not? Isn't this why you're here?" I was feeling stronger now, but my heart was still beating fast, and I couldn't control my tongue. It just... said whatever came to mind. "Worshipping something greater than yourself, something more eternal... isn't that what all men seek?"

"Careful, librarian," he said softly.

Before I could take a breath, those long fingers that I'd admired were around my throat, and his lips were pressed against mine. I fought him for an instant, but his fingers tightened around and I felt my cock straining against my jeans. My mouth opened under his and I ground my hardening cock against his powerful thigh. I could feel him smile against my lips as he claimed me. He released my throat for just a moment to pull me against the hard wall of his chest, and I could feel the swell of his own arousal pressing against my stomach. I groaned as he raked his hand down the front of my jeans. I was completely under his control... and I loved it. He rubbed harder and faster, and his tongue tangled with mine. He stole my breath and crushed me tightly against him. He devoured me, and I wanted him too. Hot and fast, I could feel my climax building, but I didn't want to.

I couldn't... not here... where anyone could see us.

But it was dark, and we were alone. I groaned deep in my throat and thrust against his hand. The man dragged his lips from mine and his voice was soft and strong in my ear as he spoke: "Yes, librarian... give in. That's what I want. You say we should worship words... but I want you to worship me."

He bit down on my throat and his teeth were sharp. I cried out in pain, and at the avalanche of sensation that crashed over me as I came... harder and faster than I had ever climaxed before. His dark chuckle filled my ears as I sagged against him.

"Wake up, librarian..."

I opened my eyes, hoping to look into those cold eyes and feel the rush they brought me... but instead, it was the bright light of morning and I was lying in a crusted puddle of my own making. I blushed hotly as I remembered my dream, and slammed my face back into my pillow.

Like a bloody teenager.

A week passed, and I did my best to forget what had happened. But my dream was hard to chase away, especially because I kept having it. Every night it was longer, and more intense, and every time his voice touched my ears I could feel myself getting hard.

I tried to bury myself in whatever work Signore de Sarno set upon my desk. Transcribing, cataloguing, repairing the bindings on books that required it. But my main focus was the copy of Dante's *Divine Comedy*. Signore de Sarno told me that it was for a patron of the library. A special request, and I put all of my care into its repair, and recorded each page with painstaking detail. It was a fine example; a handwritten, hand-stitched copy of Dante's masterwork, but it wasn't enough to keep my mind off of *him*.

"Gideon," Signore de Sarno's voice pulled me from the thick smoke of my distraction and I realized I'd been staring down at the same page for far too long. "Is it finished?"

I looked up at my mentor with a tired smile on my face. "It is."

"*Bene, molto bene*," he said. "Come, the gentleman who requested this work is here now… ready to collect it."

"Collect it?" I asked, confused. "But I thought this was to be housed in our own collection…"

"It was, but this gentleman is a great patron of the library, and he has asked to… borrow it." Signore de Sarno smiled and his eyes twinkled at me; but I was suspicious.

"Are you sure?"

"Ah, Gideon," he replied. "It is not your place to question one of our patrons, as it is not mine." He held out a square of soft leather and I took it from him warily. "He is waiting for you in the *Sala Monumentale*. Go now. He is not a patient man."

I sighed, wrapped the book in the leather and held it gently against my chest. "How will I know who he is, Signore?" I asked. "What is his name?"

"*Meilichios*… Unimportant. But you will know who he is."

Great.

"Thank you, Sigore, I'll be back as quickly as I can," I said. The last time he had sent me on a mission like this, I had been waylaid for over two hours listening to another 'great patron' of the library tell me all about how he regretted not joining the French Foreign Legion in his younger days while he made me bring out every map and battle plan I could reach… and some I couldn't. I didn't have time for anything like that today. Like any student of history, I enjoyed listening to the stories of our patrons, but there was a line that had to be drawn somewhere.

I gritted my teeth as I walked past the reception desk. Vittorio was asleep in his chair, and I slapped my hand down on the heavy wooden desk as I turned to enter the *Sala Monumentale*. "Not the time, Vittorio," I hissed.

"*Scusate!*" he hissed back sleepily.

I shook my head and picked up my pace and began to look between the stacks to find the man who was waiting for me. *No, not for me. For the book in my arms.*

I felt like a fool asking every white haired gentleman his name. "Meilichios? Signore?" But they all shook their heads. Finally, there was only one aisle left… and the one man I definitely did not have the strength to face occupied it.

Him.

CHAPTER 5 ~ HADES

I had been coming to the *Biblioteca Vallicelliana* since its ignoble beginnings as a place for educated men with dangerous points of view to gather in secrecy. Barely a mile away from Vatican City, the walls of the papal palace could be seen from the rooftop balcony. It was a daring affront, and these men of science, alchemy, and letters would toast the health of the Pope before falling to their discussions and study. I was there for it all. In secrecy of course, in the shadows... but I was there.

Pieces from my own collection had seeded the library in its early days—where else would they have acquired such dangerous pieces of literature—and I continued to donate manuscripts and scrolls when I felt the need, or when a particular topic struck my interest. The city had grown up around the library, and the power of the church had waxed and waned, but the books... the books retained their magic and their ability to inspire. I had little patience for mortals; their time on earth was so short, while their time in my domain was, well, eternal.

It was fascinating to me how much mortality, and the fear of 'disappearing' after death seemed to fuel such passionate creativity. If only they knew they would continue on... just not the way they expected.

I stared at the books in front of me, and chose one at random... but perhaps it was not random that my fingers had fallen upon it. An archaeological journal devoted to the excavation of a temple at Dodona.

Taking cues from Herodotus, Homer, and Apollonius of Rhodes, the archaeologists had sought the origins of worship of oracles, knowing that there must be more than Delphi at which penitents could worship and receive the words of the gods.

When Zeus discovered Hera's treachery, he went to Dodona. The Dione, four priestesses of the oracle, had been dedicated to him since the founding of the city and they dispensed prophecy in his name, interpreting the sound of the wind as it passed through the sacred oak tree that had grown on that spot for centuries. It sounded ridiculous. Priests and priestesses dedicated to listening to the sound of the rustling leaves... but sometimes, they were hearing my brother's true voice. Though he seemed to only lend his insight when the penitent was particularly beautiful.

But Zeus didn't go to Dodona alone. He needed a witness, and the only god qualified to accompany him was his son, Apollo.

The god of oracles and prophecy, my nephew had only vacated his seat at Delphi at his father's command. I watched as he struggled to remain neutral, but his rage at his stepmother's betrayal, and that of his own twin sister, had filled him with poison. I knew it was dangerous for them to go together to confront the oracle, but, as usual, they ignored my counsel.

I had watched from the cistern on Olympus as they approached the temple in disguise and spoke to the priest who interpreted the words of the Dione. Each moment was etched upon my memories with diamond precision. I watched the man laugh and show his blackened teeth as he told them of the prophecy. Watched as he confirmed the curse that had been laid upon the gods by the vengeful goddesses.

Hera's spite had infected Zeus' own oracle, and the words of the Dione echoed up to me, and probably in the ears of my brothers and nephews scattered across the heavens.

Argéia—Lady of the Argos. Teléia—first among women and protector of marriage. It is she who has cursed the gods. She has cut off their holy fount and rendered them barren. She has become Chérē—the divine widow.

"How can it be reversed?" Apollo had cried. "Every curse has a mirror, every prophecy an alternate..." But the priest had laughed in his face and the Dione answered him instead, their voices echoed in the oracle's chamber as they spoke with one voice:

The Lady of Curses watches you, with her dark eyes and her frozen heart. Agrotera with her bow of cold moonlight. Halosydna, the Pearl of the Oceans. Apatouros. Even the Grey-Eyed Lady.... they conspire against their husbands, their lovers, and their fathers. United against them, their words, the words of the Great Goddess, cannot be undone. When Helios pulls the moon behind his fiery chariot and the sun burns black as night, then shall this be reversed.

I watched as Zeus and Apollo struggled to control their emotions as they recognized the names and titles of their kin—sisters, wives, and daughters. The laughter of the Dione and their priest bounced off the marble columns and into the courtyard.

My own fists were clenched in rage as I realized Persephone's part in all of this. Of course it had been she who had come to Hera's aid. Who else among the goddesses was so uniquely placed to assist?

Persephone. Artemis. Amphitrite. Aphrodite. Athena. They had all done it. They had united against us, and there was nothing we could do to reverse what had been done.

Overcome with rage at the defilement of his own oracle, Zeus revealed himself in all his divine glory, and the lightning storm that split the skies over Dodona set fires that could be seen burning for hundreds of miles. The bolts he threw cracked the marble plinth beneath his colossal statue and split the great oak tree in half.

Following his father's lead, Apollo pulled the temple down on the heads of the tainted oracles and their priest, finally cutting off their laughter. It righted no wrongs, healed no hurts, reversed no curses... but it must have felt damned good.

If only the archaeologists had known what had really happened at Dodona. It wasn't the Christians who dismantled the temple and burned the sacred oak. But the mortals could keep their fictions. How would the truth be explained, anyway?

I ran my fingers over the sketch of the temple precinct. Here, where the great oak had been split by Zeus' thunderbolt. His prophecies would never whisper through those leaves again. There, where Apollo had thrown off his wool cloak and revealed his golden curls. A photo of the rubble that was once a great colossal statue of my brother. Dodona had been his favorite—his first sanctuary on the Hellenic Peninsula. And he had reduced it to rubble.

It was Persephone's hand in all of this... that was what had left me cold. It would have been easier for her to retreat to the villa I had built her in the Underworld for the duration of her time with me. Hate I could stomach with little difficulty. I would have baskets of pomegranates delivered to her doorstep for each day of our six months together, and I could bask in the knowledge that with each day that passed she would hate me more, and yet would never be free of me. But lying... *lying to my face.*

I gritted my teeth as I wondered again if I could have stopped all of this; if I could have halted Hera's revenge—

"Excuse me..." A quiet voice, almost familiar, dragged me from the deep recess of history and I felt rage at being drawn out of it so abruptly.

I slammed the book closed and turned on whatever hapless mortal had chosen to interrupt me. I had allowed myself to slide deeper into my memories than usual, and I did not regret that some of my power leapt forward as I turned. While there was no good time to disturb me, this was quite possibly one of the worst.

"What." I fairly shouted the word, and a chorus of "Shhhh!" rippled through the library in immediate response. I glowered at the aged faces that glared in my direction before looking down at the mortal who had interrupted me.

A pair of wide brown eyes stared up at me through a pair of black-rimmed glasses that were sliding down the nose of the argumentative librarian I had met in the mezzanine.

He had been bolder than any other mortal I'd met before, arguing with me over a trolley full of ancient books. *The librarian.* Over the last few weeks, he had been watching me as I stalked the halls of the *Biblioteca Vallicelliana*, and if I was reading his nervous expression and flushed cheeks correctly, he had been doing more than just watching me.

He wasn't afraid either. *That was new.*

The young man held something clutched close to his chest.

"What do you want." It wasn't a question.

"Signore de Sarno sent me to bring this to you," the young man stammered. "You requested this specific copy of the *Divine Comedy.*"

Shit. I had.

"Give it here," I snapped.

Gideon. That was his name.

The young man handed it to me carefully; his eyes were bright, and held mine unwaveringly. But as our fingers touched, I saw him flinch ever so slightly.

That was all I needed, that inch of surrender.

CHAPTER 6 ~ GIDEON

The moment I opened my mouth, I regretted it. The man turned and glared down at me as though I was a small child who had stolen something from him or touched something I shouldn't have. I swallowed thickly and tried to keep my hammering heart under control. His ghostly pale eyes were cold, and they held me prisoner.

"What?" It was almost a shout, and I fought the urge to flinch. It only took a second for the chorus of "Shhhh!" to follow the outburst, and I couldn't help but smirk just a little. If nothing else, our patrons were predictable.

"What do you want?" he snapped. I knew he wanted me to be afraid of him. I imagined he was used to people being afraid. But I wasn't. If anything, I wanted to know more about him. The remnants of my dream rushed back into my mind unbidden—the way his lips had felt on mine, and the feeling of a gathering storm that had coursed through my veins when we touched.

Get it together, you pervert; you have a job to do, and he's already pissed off.

I cleared my throat and pushed my glasses back into place. "Signore de Sarno sent me to bring this to you," I stammered. "You requested this specific copy of the *Divine Comedy*. I've completed its restoration and—"

"Give it here," he said sharply. I held his gaze and wondered what he was thinking as I held the book out to him. When our fingers touched, I felt something jolt through me, a taste of the same feeling I'd had in my dream, and I flinched ever so slightly. The stranger smiled, just a little, and I swallowed thickly.

He unwrapped the book and touched the leather cover reverently before opening it to examine my handiwork. I had spent long hours repairing the spine and re-stitching the binding as Signore de Sarno had shown me. I had come to the *Vallicelliana* as an archivist, but Signore de Sarno was quickly turning me into an antiquarian and restorer of old manuscripts. He had promised to teach me about illumination soon, a skill I was eager to learn.

"Signore de Sarno never told me your name," I said haltingly. The man looked up, as though he had forgotten I was there. He regarded me thoughtfully for a moment and then shook his head.

"Aiden, I suppose," he said.

"You suppose?"

"You wanted a name," he replied.

"But will you answer to it?"

"I don't answer to anyone."

Great job, Gideon. Greeeat job.

"I'm Gideon," I said suddenly. Unwilling to let more silence fall between us. I wanted to talk to him, I wanted to know why he had requested this book...

"I know." He didn't look up from the page this time.

"Oh... right." I remembered the conversation I'd overheard him having with Signore de Sarno in the mezzanine. They had been talking about me.

"So. Why this particular manuscript? We have several copies of Dante's entire catalogue available in the main library."

"I am aware," he said, still not meeting my eyes.

"You didn't answer my question," I said, knowing that I was

pushing against an invisible boundary. Finally, he looked up at me, his pale eyes burning coldly into mine.

"How well do you know this work?" he asked.

"Well enough. Dante completed it a year before his death; I believe he wrote it as a way to reconcile the approach of the inevitable. How wonderful would it be to believe that this version of an afterlife existed? I would take comfort in something similar."

The man raised an eyebrow. "Would you, now?"

"I don't see why not. Mankind has taken solace in similar fictions for centuries, why not this one?"

"What do you believe?"

I'd never been asked that before. Living in Rome, surrounded by the power of religion and belief, it was still difficult to explain. I'd been raised Catholic, but when I'd been able to decide for myself I wasn't entirely sure which path to take. The Church's position on what I was and how I chose to live my life didn't help matters… it was easier just to be undecided.

"I'm not sure," I said carefully. "It seems to be a very personal exploration, one I'm not sure I'm completely qualified to make yet. Alighieri was convinced that there was something more, but not a heaven, per se." I paused for just a moment, and the man's gaze didn't waver. "I don't know that I agree with him fully, and I don't know that I believe in a heaven either. I hope there's something more waiting for us when we die, but if there isn't, I think I'd be fine with that too. What matters is what we do with our time… It seems a bit selfish to believe that things will be better after we die, or that we will be able to keep doing whatever it is we were doing on earth before we're six feet under it. I don't think I'd want to do the same thing for eternity…"

I didn't know this man, how was I standing here spilling my guts to him?

"It is but Nature's way; and in the ways of Nature there is no evil to be found."

"That's Aurelius," I said with a smile. "All of the greatest leaders, even those who seem like they will never die, will, in the end, lose their lives. To believe otherwise is irrational."

"Indeed."

"You still haven't answered my question."

"Haven't I?"

"No. Why *this* particular manuscript and not one of the ten others one of the volunteers might have brought you?"

Aiden, if that was really his name, turned another page and brought it to his nose. He inhaled deeply and his eyes closed. "Because this one smells real. Like ink, sweat, and age. This book represents almost seven hundred years of speculation and discourse all inspired by a collection of words arranged in a particular order." He looked at me with a raised eyebrow. "How do you think Signore Alighieri would feel to know how his words had affected mankind?"

I blinked at him, suddenly feeling a little dizzy. "I don't know. It's a pity you can't ask him, I imagine he'd have a lot to say about it. Unfortunately, he's dead, so all we can do is guess." Aiden seemed to find that funny, which, for some reason, annoyed me.

"Indeed. And what of Virgil, do you think he would have wanted to be involved in all of this? A guide through an underworld informed by a doctrine he had never experienced? How pleased do you think he would have been to be objectified this way?"

This had taken an odd turn. He was speaking about these long dead poets as though he actually knew them. As though he could actually ask their opinions. *Was he mocking me?* I was used to being ridiculed for being a book nerd, but in the library I should have been safe from all of that. I never expected to be challenged this way by someone I had assumed was a fellow scholar.

"I always thought Virgil was a personification, a metaphor," I said stiffly. "If this is an idealized version of the underworld, I would think that Alighieri would want one of his idols to act as a guide. A perceived kindred spirit, I suppose."

"A metaphor," he snorted. "More like an expression of artistic arrogance."

"You aren't a fan?"

"Death has a funny way of bringing all mankind down to the same level," he said darkly. "After all the evils that humans visit upon each other, I tend to side with Aurelius. No man can avoid death, yet all men fear it because it means they must be brought as low as those they spurned in life."

"It's a good thing you're not in charge," I muttered.

"Oh, is it?"

"You paint a bleak picture of the afterlife. If the choice is between that and what Alighieri dreamed was possible, I'll take his fiction over yours."

Aiden closed the book and re-wrapped it in the soft leather before setting it aside and crossing his tattooed arms over his broad chest.

"You're quite bold with your opinions, librarian," he said quietly.

I swallowed hard as goosebumps prickled up my spine. *So that was what it felt like to hear him say that word aloud, spoken in that deep voice that made my mind race and my stomach churn with anticipation.*

"I don't see why I shouldn't be," I said abruptly. "Otherwise what's the point of any of this," I gestured to all the books around us. "If we just blindly follow everything that's pounded into our heads every hour of every day, none of this has any meaning." For no reason that I could explain, I could feel anger tightening in my chest, eclipsing the twisting of my stomach at being so close to him. "You must believe that, otherwise you wouldn't spend so much time here."

Aiden's eyes narrowed just a little as he looked at me.

Uh-oh.

"The pursuit of knowledge does nothing but fill mortal men with deeper regret when they look back at a life spent amongst lifeless things. All the books in the world can't change their fate. Aurelius knew this—"

"Of course he did, but he didn't despair it," I snapped.

"You've been watching me, spying on me... haven't you?"

"I..."

"Don't lie to me, librarian, I know what you've been doing." His voice was dark and dangerous as he took a step towards me. The spiral staircase that led to the mezzanine was behind me, and I stopped short as it pressed into my back.

"I should get back to work..." I said breathlessly. He was so close, and I could feel my pulse thumping in my throat.

"Oh, indeed?" he said. His words were almost a challenge and I swallowed hard, not knowing how to react.

"Yes, indeed. Now, you have your book, and if you'll excuse me…" I made to push past him, but his bulk filled the aisle, preventing my escape. The only way I could leave was up the narrow steps of the staircase behind me.

"Don't be in such a hurry, librarian," he said. "You've been watching me, I think it's only fair that I get to watch you."

"What do you mean by that?" I spun around the railing and fixed him with a glare. "I have work to do and you shouldn't be lurking here. This library is open to the public for serious study and academic pursuit—not for voyeurism."

"That makes you quite the hypocrite then."

He moved closer, and I struggled to make my feet move. The shadows in the aisle seemed to grow and flicker and I felt panic rising in my throat. *What had I gotten myself into?*

I was two steps above him on the stairs, but he still towered over me. He stared down at me and his pale eyes were cold and mocking. I knew he expected me to cower, to run away, but I couldn't move… and I didn't want to.

"Tell me the truth about why you've been watching me," he said, stepping closer again. "And don't lie."

I glared right back at him and tried to keep the tremor out of my voice. "I'm supposed to keep an eye out for suspicious people in the library. It's part of my job. You're here late, and let's be honest, you look like a sketchy asshole. You're proving me right, you know."

"Liar," he whispered. He reached out and rubbed his fingers down my throat, pausing on the pulse that thundered just under my chin. He leaned in to press an open-mouthed kiss against my jaw. Despite myself, my eyes closed and my head tilted back in an unconscious gesture of surrender. I drew in another difficult breath; the air around us was cold, something I hadn't noticed until now.

"Lonely librarian," he murmured as he kissed up my jawline. His pale fingers curled around my throat, tightening with each kiss. I gasped and struggled to breathe, my mind reeling with the sensation of his kisses and the lack of oxygen. His words were hard and mocking in my ears. "Wasting your life amongst the words of the dead. The only touch you know is the rough scratch of parchment against your skin—and your own hand against your cock when you think about me, of course."

I could feel his teeth on my earlobe, as sharp as they had been in my dream. His breath was cold as he whispered: "You've fantasized about me doing this to you, haven't you? Dominating you. Fucking you. You've dreamed about it."

My dream. I had to get away, someone would see us… My hands came up in a vain attempt to pry his fingers from around his neck and found them to be unyielding and cold. I began to scratch and shove at his chest, but I might as well have been punching stone for all the good it did.

I saw a smile cross Aiden's lips for the first time since I'd laid eyes on him, and it was filled with cruel lust, just like his eyes. His other hand came up to push my hair away from my forehead. "Admit it," he crooned. "You crave this."

My lips parted in a silent gasp as his fingers tightened on my throat again.

"You're full of shit," I managed to gasp. "I've never… given you… a second thought." *He couldn't know… I couldn't let this happen, not here.*

I watched as his eyes flitted down my body, then back up to meet my eyes. "Then why are you so hard?"

He released me suddenly, and my knees gave way beneath me; I crumpled onto the steps, coughing and clutching my throat. He lifted one long, pale finger to his lips in a taunting shushing gesture. I raised one of my own in another gesture entirely.

"Get out of here before I call the *polizia*, creep," I muttered. I could feel my skin throbbing where his fingers had been and hoped that they wouldn't turn into bruises. "Unless you're willing to tell me who you really are, and what you're really doing here, I have work to do."

"But librarian," he purred. "Surely you'll want to take care of your… little problem first."

He crouched down and trailed one finger up the stiff curve of the erection that strained against my jeans. I shuddered beneath his touch and smacked his hand away.

"Fuck," I muttered and dragged a hand through my hair in frustration—there was no way I could walk out of this with my dignity intact, one way or the other. There were people in the mezzanine, people on the main floor, and I didn't know what I'd do if I ran into Emilie or one of the other volunteers...

"Go on, *bell'uomo*," Aiden whispered. He seemed to be enjoying my discomfort immensely. "Take care of yourself."

"You're unbelievable! I'm not doing anything, especially in front of you!" I snapped.

He shushed me again and received another obscene gesture in return. "Keep your voice down, signore—you wouldn't want anyone to find you like this, would you? The respected archivist of the *Biblioteca Vallicelliana*, undone?"

I glared up at him from my slumped position on the staircase, my breathing still uneven and slightly pained. Between the tousled hair and the red marks on my neck, the unmistakable curve of my erection in these goddamned tight pants, I must have looked utterly debauched already. But an even bigger problem was that the prospect of being caught was only arousing me more—and, worse, he seemed to know exactly what I was thinking.

"Besides," he murmured, leaning against the railing and glancing at his watch, as if the entire thing already bored him. "You've watched me without my permission before. I'm just returning the favor. Touch yourself, or I'll draw attention to us. Perhaps the volunteers are looking for you, or the dear Signore... Then you'll have more than one pair of eyes to worry about."

I tried to snarl at him, but I couldn't hide my growing excitement, or the painful throb of my cock against my jeans. *Fuck it.* His pale eyes never left mine as, angrily, I unbuttoned my pants and slipped out my cock. I started to jerk it with fast, careless strokes. If I could get this over and done with quickly, I could hide in the archive room again until it was time to leave and I could forget all about it... forget all about *him*.

"What's the rush, librarian?" he mocked me. He wetted his lips as he watched my hand move up and down the thick length of my cock. "Does the thought of being discovered really arouse you this much? Or is it being forced to touch yourself against your will that has you leaking all over yourself like a desperate virgin? I bet you'd love for me to tie you up and take whatever I wanted from you, denying your pleasure to fulfill my own. Wouldn't you?"

"You fucking wish," I hissed—but he didn't fail to notice how my strokes quickened at the very suggestion.

With a swiftness that caught me off guard, he was suddenly standing unbearably close to me, straddling me, his crotch level with my face. My hand faltered as he freed his own cock and stroked it quickly to hardness, mere inches from my quivering lips. I was hungry for him, and I knew he could see it in my eyes.

"I know the darkest fantasies in the hearts of men," he whispered. "I know you'd love to suck me off right now, right here in your precious library—you'd try to pretend you didn't want it, of course, proud fool that you are, but when I asked a second or third time, you'd stop protesting. And when I pushed it to the back of your throat, cutting off your air once more, and kept it there until you choked, you'd come harder than you've ever come in your life, and afterwards you'd thank me for it. Or am I wrong?"

With some difficulty, I managed to drag my eyes back up to his face. I was so close to a furious climax, one that felt like it had been building inside me for the better part of a year, and his eyes reflected the furious need in mine.

"Dead wrong," I said through gritted teeth—his cold smile told me that I was a terrible liar.

With one hand still lazily stroking his cock, he used the other to grab my throat and squeeze. He dug his fingers into the same tender spots he'd found before, expertly controlling me. That did it; with a cry that was stifled to a breathless gasp by his choking grasp, I came… hard. It filled my hand and spattered over my dark shirt and jeans, unmistakable and shameful. As though he'd planned it this way.

Bastard.

He kept his firm grip on my throat, hard and almost comforting, until the last aftershock had trembled through me. When he released me, he rubbed a hand down my cheek, almost gently. I drew in a gasping breath, the blood rushing to my cheeks when I saw what had happened. But in spite of my embarrassment—or, maybe, because of it—my cock betrayed me, twitching with the first hints of fresh arousal.

"Now beg me," he said. "Beg me to put my cock in your mouth."

"Fuck off," I spat, panting and hanging on to the metal railing for dear life.

He shrugged. "Your loss."

"Wait…" I shook my head and looked away, ashamed and annoyed in equal measure. "Fine."

"Beg. Tell me how much you want it."

"I'm not fucking begging you!"

"Keep your voice down, librarian," he purred. "At least say please. We are civilized men after all, are we not?"

I gritted my teeth, but my mouth was hungry for him. "Okay, please. Please can I suck your cock?"

He smirked, and in a move quick enough to disorient me, Aiden had stepped away from me and tucked his hard cock back into his pants.

"No," he said, and then turned and headed down the stairs. He collected the leather-wrapped book and disappeared into the shadows before I could formulate another word. I groaned and leaned my head against the staircase railing. My heart pounded in my throat and my cock throbbed…

"I know the darkest fantasies in the hearts of men…"

I shivered at the delicious way his words had made me feel. It was always the quiet ones, the ones you least suspected that were the most willing to surrender to those desires. I'd never been with anyone who could give me what I wanted. But Aiden… it was as if he'd already known. As if he'd peered inside my dreams and brought them to life.

I shook my head and dragged myself to my feet. I was a mess. All I could do was tuck my cock away and sneak through the mezzanine and hope that no one would see me… I'd had enough of people watching me for today. It might have been my imagination, but I could hear Aiden's sardonic laughter floating through the corridors. The sound gave me goosebumps and made my cock twitch in my pants.

I wondered if he knew what he'd done, what he'd awakened in me. Something told me that he knew exactly what he was doing, and I was going to have to watch my back.

CHAPTER 7 ~ HADES

"Brother, we were beginning to wonder if you were ever coming home," Poseidon greeted me with a smile as I approached the throne room. We never used the blasted thing anymore, and I didn't understand Zeus' petulant insistence at keeping them at all. Mine was made of black basalt, large and imposing, but I hadn't touched it in centuries.

"Zeus sent a command, how could I refuse my brother?"

"It's what I'd expect of you," Poseidon said. "I told him it was foolish to send the message at all."

I smirked; he wasn't wrong. "Of all the commands I've ever ignored, I would be the worst of all brothers to refuse to acknowledge this one."

Poseidon nodded. "Not to mention we'd never hear the end of it."

"How many others are here?"

"Most... some I haven't seen in a very long time. Hermes has been busy."

"I'm sure he has," I said. "Keep in mind that you haven't spent much time here either, brother. Just because you've found something to keep you here doesn't make you any different from them. We've all been avoiding this... problem in our own ways."

Poseidon chuckled just a little, which surprised me; evidently, finding Brooke had changed my usually sodden brother more than I had expected. "You've been spending quite a bit of time among the mortals yourself," he said. "Should I tell Zeus that you might have found something... or someone? Or shall we wait until after the birth?"

"I don't know what you're talking about," I snapped. I could hear the murmur of voices echoing down the marble hall. We were late. If we missed it, I knew I would never hear the end of it.

"I think you do," Poseidon said, quickening his pace to catch up with me. "It's like we've both said, brother. When you find your spark, you'll know. Even you won't be able to avoid this prophecy, no matter how hard you—"

"And where is your mortal?" I interrupted him. "Have you kept them out of my library as I instructed?"

"You left Cerberus off his chains," Poseidon said stiffly. "Of course they've stayed out. Besides, they're not mortal anymore; you'd do well to remember that fact. They're Olympians now, and should be treated with the respect they deserve."

"Respect?" I sneered. "They are only immortal because of a loophole in a curse... nothing more. If you hadn't interrupted their simple mortal lives, they would never have known any different."

"And we would never have defeated Hera's curse."

"We haven't defeated it, you arrogant fool. We've only sidestepped it."

Poseidon opened his mouth to say something else, but a rush of wind interrupted him as Hermes appeared beside us.

"Have I missed it?" he asked quickly.

Poseidon looked surprised. "I didn't know you'd left again," he said.

"I forgot something," my nephew replied. "Ares is here, have you seen him?"

"Ares? I didn't expect him to be here until after the birth." Poseidon's confusion seemed to deepen and I wondered what had happened while I had been away.

"No, uncle, he was one of the first to arrive. Hephaestus, too."

I couldn't help but laugh, and the sound bounced off the marble columns. Hermes made a face, and I relished his discomfort a little more than I'd anticipated. "What a happy family reunion this will be," I said cruelly. "Wouldn't Hera be pleased to see us united once more."

"Don't say her name," Hermes hissed. "She's watching us."

"You sound very sure of yourself, nephew," I said. "Have you seen her on your travels? Come, tell us all the news. How is my dear sister?"

"Hades, be careful," Poseidon said. "If Zeus hears you—"

"What? What will he do?" I challenged. I glared down at my brother and my nephew and they both shifted nervously, not knowing what to say in reply. "That's what I thought."

I swept into the room and was immediately wrapped in a pair of muscular arms. Hephaestus' presence on Olympus was a rare sight, indeed, and I couldn't recall the last time I had spoken to the god of the forge.

"Uncle," he welcomed me warmly and shook my hand with an iron grip. His palm was as hot as the heart of the volcano he made his palace in. My fiery nephew hadn't changed very much over the centuries. Still eager to please, and as hot-blooded as Ares. If Hera hadn't injured him at such a young age, I had no doubt that he would have rivaled his elder brother in ferocity and power.

His long red hair, woven into a tight braid and secured by a thick band of gold, fell over his shoulder. It was the only finery he wore, but I was surprised that he had kept it. A wedding gift from Aphrodite… if I had been in his place, I would have cast it into the heart of Mount Aetna long ago.

"You are just in time," he said eagerly. "Father has just announced that the time is near."

"So it would seem," I said dryly. The room was full of ethereal light, and delicate draperies fluttered softly in the light breeze that blew through the room. Zeus was doing his best to make everything comfortable and relaxing, if not for his mortal's benefit, then for his own.

The sheer draperies also served as a protective screen between the other gods and the birthing couch. I could see Cameron, stretched out upon it; a thin sheet covered his torso and I could see the curve of his belly clearly. Apollo stood nearby with Zeus, and Poseidon's mortal was seated on a chair next to the couch, and bathed Cameron's head with a wet cloth.

"I see Brooke has settled into his place on Olympus quite comfortably," I murmured to Poseidon.

"Shut your mouth," he snapped.

"Always second, brother."

"I said shut up." Poseidon's hands curled into fists and I smiled down at my brother. He was so easy to manipulate. That would never change.

"How long until Brooke is lying under Apollo's hands?" I asked quietly.

The look in Poseidon's eyes told me everything I needed to know and I chuckled quietly. "You are terrible at keeping secrets, brother. When did you plan to tell Zeus?"

"Shut. Up," he said through gritted teeth.

"Hush, now, our brother has something to say," I said soothingly as Zeus stepped through the curtain blocking our view. He held up his hands and smiled out at the immortals that had gathered.

"My brothers… my sons… Olympians, all. Welcome. I can't even begin to tell you how important this day is." I coughed loudly, interrupting him. Zeus fixed me with a stern glare, electricity snapping in his gray eyes. Next to me Hephaestus chuckled, but quieted at a nudge from Hermes. "Today we take back Olympus for ourselves… today we send a message to the goddesses who cursed us."

There was a groan from behind the curtains and I saw Apollo bend over the couch. Brooke was holding Cameron's hand tightly. Out of the corner of my eye, I saw Poseidon shift uncomfortably, and Ares stepped forward.

I turned my attention to my nephew… I hadn't expected that reaction from Ares, or any reaction at all.

"When my child is born, the first of the New Olympians, you will see for yourselves that there is a chance for us to take back what was stolen from us. A new god or goddess will join our pantheon, and Olympus will once again be a place of joy."

The sound of Cameron's groan filled the air again, and Zeus' expression took on a shade of panic. He disappeared behind the curtain and a hush fell over the room as we listened to the ruler of Olympus comfort his mortal. Soothing words that were soon drowned out by Cameron's cries of pain and fear.

Beside me, Poseidon's hands clenched into fists, his knuckles white with the intensity of his grip. I knew he was thinking about Brooke, and what he would have to go through. I shifted my gaze to Ares, who seemed to be in a similar amount of distress. I would have to remind myself to speak to my nephew after this was all over…

"Don't worry brother, your spark is immortal now, just like Zeus'… soon this will all be just a memory." I had meant for my words to be soothing, but Poseidon's furious answering glare was an indication of how terrible I was at soothing.

There was another cry, and Zeus' triumphant bellow. And then a different sound… one I had not heard in centuries. The squall of a newborn god.

The child's cries echoed off the marble columns and the draperies fluttered in a fresh wind that swept through the room, one that smelled of flowers and summer rain. I let out a breath I didn't realize I'd been holding as the room erupted in cheers and applause.

It was Apollo's face I saw next; his expression was unreadable as he pushed aside the curtain to reveal Cameron lying upon the birthing couch.

The former mortal looked tired and pained, and his cheeks were stained with tears, but he glowed with pride… as did my brother. Zeus took a swaddled bundle from Cameron's arms and rose from his seat next to the couch.

"Behold… the first of the New Olympians." He held the child aloft, and I did my best not to roll my eyes at his dramatics. "Behold… Alkira, Goddess of the Spring Winds."

"I'm so glad he took my advice and named the child himself," I murmured to Poseidon. My brother looked at me in confusion, but Zeus seemed to have heard me and his expression hardened just a little.

"Brothers... my sons. See for yourselves, Hera's curse holds no power in Olympus now." Zeus paused, making eye contact with each and every immortal in the room as his words vibrated off the marble columns. "If you wish to rebuild Olympus as I do, you will go forth and find your spark... the goddesses have been arrogant in their revenge for too long."

"How do we know this is not just an anomaly?" someone cried. I did not see the speaker, but Zeus cradled his child against his chest and stroked her cheek gently before replying.

"This is not an anomaly..." he said softly. "My child is not an anomaly. She is an Olympian, just like you. These sparks... these mortals. You will be drawn to them. At first, you won't be able to explain it, you might even resist the pull of that attraction. But these mortals have been placed in your path for a reason... one that even I cannot explain."

Poseidon stepped through the curtains and took Brooke by the hand to lead him forward. Cameron was sleeping on the couch, exhausted from his ordeal. Apollo stood behind the couch, a protective presence, and a reminder that though this was a happy occasion, the goddesses still posed a very real threat.

Zeus smiled as his brother joined him. "More than my own child, we will soon welcome another to our number... my niece or nephew will soon be born. Another testament to the power of our sparks. The power of the prophecy deciphered by Hades and delivered to all of you. You have chosen not to believe it... you have argued against me. But now, now you can no longer deny it."

Poseidon pulled Brooke's tunic aside to reveal the swell of his belly. There was a collective sigh as the gods beheld the new pregnancy—another immortal waiting to be born. The mortal blushed and covered his growing stomach with his hands. Poseidon's indulgent smile made my own stomach turn.

Was it going to be like this every time? Some saccharine ceremony for every birth, every pregnancy? It was almost too much to bear.

I felt an elbow nudge into my ribs. "When will it be your turn, uncle?"

"What?"

Hephaestus, I had almost forgotten about him.

"When will we see you standing there to present your child?"

"Me?" I scoffed. "No, nephew, this prophecy is not for me."

Zeus' red-headed son smiled crookedly at me. "Are you so sure? If I were to see you with a child in your arms, it would give me some hope."

"I am not here to give you hope, Hephaestus. Prophecies, and those who believe in them are fools. If you think that the goddesses have been defeated… that Hera will turn a blind eye to this defiance…" I paused, realizing that the eyes of all the immortals in the room were turned upon me. Including those of my brothers.

I didn't give a shit about angering Zeus. I knew my place, and it was in the underworld, in the confines of my library. Not in the nursery. Let them have their sparks… their mortals. I was the only eternal god. The eldest… the *chthonian*.

"Hades!" Zeus' shout reverberated off the marble walls and the child in his arms began to cry. Cameron stirred on the couch and Brooke rushed to his side.

I was done with this. I swept from the room before my brother could lecture me, and the shadows that accompanied me left a darkness in my wake that only faded when I allowed it.

I strode through the colonnade towards the marble stairs that led down to my library. I could hear Cerberus' growl as I approached and I smiled at the familiar sound.

"There now, your job is done," I said softly. Cerberus, ever faithful, ceased his growling as soon as he smelled me; ash and bone… comforting and natural. This was my home, and the silence was comforting. Poseidon had told me once that the quiet was overwhelming, almost oppressive… but this was what I craved.

I poured myself a goblet of wine and took a long drink. After today, Olympus would never be the same. The sound of children—their laughter, their tears… their cries of sorrow and joy. Olympus would never be quiet again. This library would be my only sanctuary.

The face of the librarian at the *Biblioteca Vallicelliana* flashed across my mind. Specifically the expression on his face when he had finally submitted to me on those spiral stairs… it had been delicious. I hadn't believed that it could be possible, to find someone who would bend to my will in such a way—to challenge me without fear. Persephone had never given in to my proclivities, and others, well, they had not survived it.

But Gideon. Gideon was different. I wanted to test his boundaries; I wanted to see how much it would take for him to writhe and beg me to take him. My brothers had made too much noise about how they had known their sparks when they found them. But I refused to believe it. I could not deny that I had felt something when my lips had touched Gideon's skin. A gathering storm in my chest, the billowing of clouds in my mind… and a cold rush, as of the Acheron overflowing its banks.

What if I was lying to myself?

Did I owe it to my brothers to discover the truth of it? If I was meant to be a part of this rebirth of Olympus, I would have known it by now. I was the elder brother… I should have been first. I slammed the cup down and watched the dark liquid splash onto the floor. Cerberus, ever helpful, lapped up the mess greedily and I reached down to fondle one set of his dark ears.

"We don't need any company… do we?" I murmured as I sank into one of the great chairs Hephaestus had made for me. A fire crackled in the great hearth in front of me. The dark flames gave off no heat, but for some reason, the flickering core gave me no comfort.

It wouldn't be long before Zeus would come stomping down those marble steps to scold me for ruining his pompous presentation ceremony.

I had to return to Rome. I couldn't stay here.

Cerberus rested his heads on my knee and looked up at me expectantly. I stroked each muzzle gently, and smiled down at him. "You've been cooped up here too long, my friend. Would you like to see Rome again?"

One of Cerberus' heads raised a canine eyebrow as the middle one let out a small yip of excitement. His thick tail thumped against the marble paving stones and I smiled wider.

"That's what I thought."

CHAPTER 8 ~ GIDEON

I thought about Aiden (if that really was his name) constantly for the next week. I went out of my way to find books and manuscripts that supported my position on Alighieri's approach to the afterlife. What I really should have been doing was tackling the pile of books on my desk, but I needed to do something else—anything else—to distract me from thinking about him; about what had happened in that narrow spiral staircase. Anyone could have seen us, and part of me had wanted to be discovered.

My cock twitched and I tried to focus on the book in front of me. I'd read the spine half a dozen times, and still not registered what it was or where it should be catalogued. I imagined Aiden standing behind me, chuckling at how flustered I was… at how easily I was distracted thinking about him.

Ridiculous.

He hadn't been back to the library in days, but I didn't know how many had passed. Was he avoiding me? Should I be feeling more ashamed than I actually was for how badly I'd wanted to act on my dreams? *Was this even about me? Ugh.*

Signore de Sarno had been curiously talkative since I'd given Aiden the book he'd ordered, and he seemed particularly excited about a large package that had arrived that needed his special attention.

"Come, Gideon," he said one day. "*Guarda qui*, I have a challenge for you." He beckoned me over to his ink-stained desk so I could look more closely at the contents of the package. My mouth dropped open as he unwrapped the books.

"But, Signore, they're burned... how are we supposed to repair these?" I asked. "Some of these are too damaged... who would do such a thing?"

Signore de Sarno chuckled and set one of the damaged books gently in front of himself. His desk had come from the scriptorium of a monastery that had been destroyed by an earthquake decades ago, and it was a particular quirk of his to sit at this desk to work on his most important, or challenging in this case, projects. He had never let me sit at it, but I hoped that would change one day...

"From what I have been told, this was the revenge of a jealous wife... she accused him of loving his books more than he loved her..."

"Let me guess, she was right?"

My mentor chuckled and opened the book. I gasped to see the damage the fire had done. "What are we supposed to do? I can re-stitch a broken spine and repair split leather, but this..."

"Our patron has asked us to become monks, Gideon," he replied with a smile.

"What does that mean," I asked with a raised eyebrow. "I'm not sure I'm cut out for monastic life..."

Signore de Sarno laughed heartily and clapped me on the back. "No, no, Gideon. You are meant for much bigger things. What I mean to say is that our patron has requested that the manuscripts be copied and illuminated, just as the monks used to do."

I stared at the pile of scorched books with wide eyes. "All of them?"

"*Come dici*," he said with a smile. "There are many long nights ahead of us, I think. Enough to keep even you out of trouble." He winked at me and I felt my cheeks heating just a little. *What did he mean by that? Oh, god, what if he'd seen—*

I cleared my throat and tried to bring the subject back to the books. To say that I wasn't looking forward to this challenge would be a lie; it was just... daunting. "Who is our patron, signore? You've never said his name."

"Signore Agesander," he replied. "He comes from a very old family... ancient you might say. They have been great patrons of the library since the very beginning." Signore de Sarno set his glasses upon his wild white hair and leaned back in his chair. He gestured vaguely at the records that lined the walls around us. "If you go back in the *Vallicelliana's* archives, you will see that there is an Agesander present at every secret meeting... and every formal one too. When I started my apprenticeship here, I was younger than you, Gideon. I knew his grandfather at the very end, his father, and now the torch has passed to him. It is very rare to find a family so dedicated to something so richly rewarding for all mankind..."

"Yes, very rare," I murmured.

Signore de Sarno and I spent many long hours poring over the books and discussing how best to approach the restoration of those that could be saved, and the painstaking work that would have to go into the duplication of the others. I was given three to repair; their covers were only lightly scorched, and it would take some time, but I would be able to bring the leather back to its original luster and re-lay the gold leaf that had been damaged.

"These books... they are all from the same library?" I asked unnecessarily as the signore locked the archive room door.

"*Ovviamente*," he replied with a chuckle. "Did you notice the subject matter of each book as well?"

I nodded. "The French translation of Ovid's *Metamorphoses* is the one that intrigues me the most. I think I'll be able to repair it without too much difficulty. The pages that are the most heavily damaged seem to only be marred with soot and can be easily cleaned..."

"*Buona. Molto bene.* He will be glad to hear it."

"When will *he* be back at the library, signore?" I asked, blushing just a little as he turned a curious eye upon me. "I'm just curious about the fire, and his collection. These are very fine books… and if his family has been a part of the *Vallicelliana* since the earliest days… I can only imagine what his personal library looks like."

The signore smiled and shook his head. *"La troppa curiosità spinge l'uccello nella rete,"* he said as he shook a finger at me. I blinked at him for a moment, trying to translate what he'd said in my head. He noticed my confusion and patted me on the shoulder. "Curiosity killed the cat, my young friend."

I laughed awkwardly and lifted my bag onto my shoulder. "Right. I'm still slow with idioms, signore." *Was that supposed to be a warning? What did he know that he wasn't telling me?*

We parted ways at the black door once more and I watched the signore make his way through the piazza towards the river before turning towards my apartment. I walked the same way every day, why should tonight be any different? But something was pulling me towards the river too, and before I knew what was happening, my feet had carried me along the same path as my mentor and I stood at the edge of the St. Angelo Bridge, staring out over the Tiber and at the walls of the holy fortress of Vatican City.

Most people I knew complained about the smell of the river, but they'd never smelled downtown Boston on a hot day. It had been too long since I'd sat near the water, and it was obviously high time I corrected that. The sun was setting slowly over my shoulder and the brightly painted sky was reflected in the river. I sank down onto the stones of the walkway with something like a happy sigh and let my feet dangle over the edge. The soles of my shoes barely touched the water and I let them float there lightly and watched the ripples disturb the surface.

It was strangely quiet for a weeknight. Usually the river was busy with boats and barges, and the streets full of honking cars, the buzz of mopeds, and the occasional roar of a motorcycle ripping through the Vatican City precinct.

I pulled a small book out of my bag and opened it to a page I'd marked before I left the library. I had been telling Signore de Sarno the truth; the copy of *Metamorphoses* that had found its way onto my restoration desk intrigued me.

> *Aphrodite, from her mountain throne, saw him and clasped her swift-winged son, and said: 'Eros, my child, my warrior, my power, take those sure shafts with which you conquer all, and shoot your speedy arrows to the heart of the great god to whom the last lot fell when the three realms were drawn. Your majesty subdues the gods of heaven and sea... Why should Tartarus lag behind?*

"I suppose I should not be surprised to find you with your nose buried in a book even outside of your usual duties."

I looked up and came face to face with the muzzle of a very large, very black dog. I tried to slide back, but I was stopped by a deep growl that came from behind me. I froze and stared up at the black shape above me and gritted my teeth as I was able to place the chuckle that followed my discomfort. Three black dogs, tall and lean, examined me closely, and I tried to ignore the chills that ran up my spine as their cold breath hit my skin. I couldn't help the way my heart pounded when the red light of the sunset illuminated Aiden's face.

"Are you following me now?" I asked, keeping a wary eye on the dogs who hadn't paused in their examination of me. They were taller than any dog I'd ever seen before. Their coats were black and shone like obsidian—blacker than anything in this world.

I'd never owned a dog, but I'd always wanted one, and the temptation to touch them, regardless of how terrifying they were, was almost impossible to deny. I reached out a tentative hand towards the pointed muzzle nearest to me. If its massive jaws snapped over my fingers, I'd never repair a manuscript ever again, but the temptation was too great. *I had to know.*

La troppa curiosità spinge l'uccello nella rete—Signore de Sarno would laugh at me now. But I didn't care.

The hellhound, for it very well could have been, sniffed at my hand, a growl bubbling in its wide chest.

"Careful..." Aiden's voice was cold and I was frozen in place until the massive dog surprised me by stepping closer and bathing my face with a broad pink tongue. The second dog, just as massive as the first, whined happily and jumped at me, snuffling into my hair and the collar of my shirt. I yelped at the coldness of his nose. The third dog tugged the book out of my hand, growling playfully as he held it in his massive jaws.

"Hey!" I laughed as the first two dogs crashed into me, licking and barking happily. Through the tangle of canine limbs I looked up to see Aiden as he took the book out of his dog's mouth and opened it to the page I'd been reading. He looked at it with a raised eyebrow and then back at me. A smile flitted across his face and it chilled me just a little. He looked surprised, but I didn't know what had caused it.

He pulled the dogs away, but they seemed eager for my affection and I rubbed each set of dark ears. "What's his name?" I asked, pointing at the largest of the three.

In reply, Aiden held up the book his dog had stolen from me. "Why are you reading this?"

I scrambled to my feet and pulled my bag over my shoulder. "Why not? Who are you to judge what I choose to read in my private time... besides, I'm working on the books you sent us and I was reminded that I hadn't read any Ovid since college." I tried to snatch the book out of his hand, but his grip was tight. I wrestled with him briefly until he finally released it and I shoved the book deep into my bag.

I glared at him and tugged my jacket tighter around my chest. "Are you going to say anything about what happened?"

"*What* happened?" he said.

I gritted my teeth and narrowed my eyes. One of the dogs licked my palm, distracting me from my anger just a little. "You know exactly what happened."

"Ah, that."

"Yes, that!"

"What do you want me to say?"

"I..." my words froze in my throat as his pale eyes held mine unwaveringly.

"You want me to say that I've been thinking about you... that I haven't been able to get you out of my mind... is that it, librarian?"

I swallowed thickly. *That was exactly what I wanted to hear, but I'd never say it. He didn't deserve that.*

"I see," he said. His smile was cruel and sent a shiver up my spine. The last time I'd seen that smile I'd been choking under his grip and loving every second of it.

"You didn't answer my question," I said.

"Didn't I?"

"No." I pointed at the dogs. "What are their names?"

"Spot," he said.

"Seriously... and the other two?"

Aiden whistled through his teeth at the dogs, and they pulled themselves reluctantly away from me. "Spot," he said over his shoulder.

"That's stupid," I shouted at his back. He didn't turn, but one of the dogs looked back at me, his tongue lolling out of his mouth in a goofy expression that made me smile. A terrifying animal when I'd first met him; nothing but a puppy looking for affection after all.

It was almost dark, and I knew I should go home, but running into Aiden like that had set my teeth on edge. I wanted him... but this one-sided bullshit wasn't my style. I didn't have a problem pursuing, but there had to be something there. *But was there?*

I was almost home, and my path took me past a narrow street full of bars that only opened after the sun went down. I usually passed quickly, but tonight when the seats were full and the lights blazed warmly, I felt the pull a little more strongly.

"Gideon! Gideon! Oh. My. God!"

A full tackle accompanied the familiar shout as Emilie flew out of one of the bars and flung herself at me. She wrapped her arms around my shoulders and squeezed me tightly. "You can't escape, I've caught you!" she cried triumphantly. "Now you have to come and have a drink with me!"

"Fine... fine, fine... one drink," I laughed. Emilie's friends cheered their approval as she dragged me back to their table and I was introduced to a gaggle of people whose names I would never remember under torture. Laughing faces and bad jokes, accents from all over the world. Backpackers, I assumed, people she knew from her travels and maybe even a roommate or former lover or three. Guys and girls, they all crowded around to ask me questions.

"What do you do?"

"How long have you lived in Rome?"

"Don't you miss American food?"

I answered them as quickly as I could, but their questions overlapped my responses and soon the noise level had all but drowned out any other conversation as the speakers in the bar blared the newest (or maybe I was just out of touch) EuroPop hits to encourage patrons to dance and howl lyrics they could barely pronounce, let alone understand.

"So, Gideon... tell me about that guy." Emilie's voice cut through the noise like a dagger and I tried to focus on her.

"What? What guy?"

Her eyes were dark, almost as black as her hair in the strange light of the bar, and I blinked to try and clear my vision.

"You know what guy," she said with a sly smile. She slid closer to me and pushed a perspiring glass of dark beer towards me. "The one with the tattoos... do you think he's tattooed everywhere?"

I wish I knew.

I laughed instead. "That's a silly question. And I still don't know what you're talking about."

"You know exactly who I'm talking about. Vittorio told me he's a patron of the library... very rich, very influential. Very sexy," she said with a wink.

"Uhhh... I guess," I said warily.

"Don't be shy, Gideon, you can tell me."

"There's nothing to tell," I said. *That was a lie.* I took a quick sip of the beer in front of me and Emilie smiled.

"Come on, Gid... Vittorio told me everything."

I raised an eyebrow and pushed the beer away. "Oh, really?"

Emilie nodded. "Yup. He's seen you two talking... How did he describe it? Oh, yes... a heated argument. A lover's quarrel perhaps? You can tell me, Gideon. You know how much I love juicy gossip. A rich patron dallying with a lowly librarian? It's practically ripped straight out of a romance novel! Except, he's married and you're... well... you're you."

I bristled at that. "What's that supposed to mean?"

"Don't take it personally," she said in a rush. "I just mean that it all sounds a little... ridiculous, don't you think?"

It did sound ridiculous. But I didn't need to hear that from her to know that it was true. That same word had floated through my mind repeatedly over the last few weeks. *One strange event after another... all of them with one common denominator, they were all ridiculous.*

"Has he said anything to you?" Emilie asked, breaking through my trance once again.

"Said anything?" I swallowed hard and hoped she wouldn't notice. *He'd said lots of things... things I didn't dare repeat.* "Like what?"

Emilie's black eyes sparkled in the dim light. "I dunno... anything weird? Rich people are always so eccentric. He looks like the eccentric type, don't you think?"

I shook my head. "Nope... sorry to disappoint you. Nothing weird. He's just a guy who likes books."

Emilie pouted just a little and opened her mouth to say something else, but before she could speak, I felt a cold hand close over my arm.

CHAPTER 9 - HADES

I hadn't meant to find Gideon by the river, but something had pulled me there... something that wasn't Cerberus—although he did his fair share of pulling along the way. It would be a lie to say that I hadn't thought about the librarian while I'd been on Olympus. In fact, during the birth of the first goddess of the new Pantheon, I'd been thinking about how much I wanted to bend Gideon over a stack of books and make him scream while he begged for my cock. I wondered what my dear brother Zeus would have to say about that.

Cerberus leaned his weight against my leg and I reached down to rub the ears of his middle head. "And you, you damned traitor, what was all that puppy shit about?" Cerberus' third head licked my wrist and panted happily. "Unbelievable." The terrifying guard of the gates of the Underworld (and sometimes my library) reduced to a snuffling, drooling mess because of a mortal. "Have you even smelled a mortal before?" I scolded him gently.

Cerberus' tail thumped on the marble stones and he stared at me with three sets of red eyes. Three tongues lolled out of three vicious mouths filled with teeth, sharp and shining. "Unbelievable," I muttered again. "That's the last time we go for a walk on earth. If you're going to act like that with every mortal we meet, we'll never get anything done."

I threw three large chunks of bleeding, raw meat in front of my demonic dog and watched his three heads growl and snap over their supper. I thought about Gideon as I watched Cerberus eat.

Gideon had been defiant, challenging me over how I had left him in the library. He was stronger than he gave himself credit for, that much was certain, and he also had a mouth that was going to get him into some serious trouble. *Maybe that's what he wanted.*

Maybe that's what I wanted.

I had taken the rights of a husband when Persephone was bound to my kingdom, but my ex-wife was a goddess more suited to flowers, candles, and gentle lovemaking. My cravings were darker and more… primal. I'd bedded my share of mortals over the centuries; they'd been terrified of me, which made it all too easy. But, unlike my brothers, none of them were able to slake my lust for something more. But Gideon… Gideon was different. Gideon was a challenge. I chuckled as I remembered how he had blushed in the gathering twilight as he stared up at me.

It was always the quiet ones who harbored the most secrets.

"Uncle? Uncle, are you down here?"

Cerberus growled over his meal and I gritted my teeth. Ever since this damned prophecy had come to light, I'd seen more of my family than I ever wanted to. Interruptions right and left. No peace! And then the children… "Tartarus be damned, will it ever end?"

"Uncle!" There was a slap of leather sandals on the marble stairs that lead up to Olympus and my nephew appeared. His long red hair bounced on his shoulders and his blue eyes were wild and bright.

"What?" I roared. Hephaestus skidded to a halt and leaned against the wall of the library. The god of the forge was a large lad, almost as tall as me and twice as broad. Centuries spent bashing out shields and armor had etched out every single muscle on his bare torso. He was always shirtless, my nephew, but the heat of the volcano where he made his home radiated off his burnished skin, so I couldn't really comment on his state of undress. I just liked it a little colder.

"My father is asking when you're coming to see the baby," he said with a grin. My nephew wasn't stupid, and neither was my brother. "She's quite remarkable," he continued. "Only a few days old and already making little wind storms in her nursery."

"How thrilling," I drawled. Hephaestus smiled and pushed his hair out of his eyes. He had always been my favorite of my nephews, if only because of how his mother had mistreated him. He still bore the scars of Hera's wrath from so many centuries ago, but his limp was only noticeable if you knew to look for it.

Cerberus, finished ripping apart his meal, licked his chops and greeted my nephew by placing his giant paws upon Hephaestus' shoulders and licking his hairy face with all three tongues. Hephaestus laughed and pushed the massive hound aside.

"Is my father right?" he asked as he wiped his face with a broad, callused hand. "Is there a spark waiting out there for each of us?"

I let out a long breath. "If your father is to be believed, there is a spark out there for each and every member of the Pantheon, even that lecherous goat you call nephew."

"You don't believe it?"

"I have to believe it, nephew," I said sharply. "The evidence is in Olympus at this very moment, no doubt screaming her divine lungs out." I shook my head. "Your mother and her minions were very busy on earth, and that means there is a chance for all of us."

"Even you, uncle," Hephaestus said quietly.

I snorted in derision. "Death needs no consort," I spat.

Hephaestus shrugged and reached down to stroke Cerberus' long noses. "As you say... but it would be a shame if Olympus were filled with the sounds of children and you were left down here alone."

"Would it?" I said stiffly.

"I think so," he replied. "When my father married me to Aphrodite, I was thrilled... how could I not be? The most beautiful goddess was mine forever—"

"It was a cruel joke," I interrupted him sharply. I didn't need to hear this story *again*.

Hephaestus nodded. "And punishment for her. But the prophecy...

it makes me believe that there is a mortal somewhere that was made for me. They don't have to be perfect; they just have to be perfect for me. No tricks, no punishments. If I could find that, it would make all these centuries of pain worthwhile." He fixed his bright cobalt eyes on me, his expression wistful. "Don't you wish you could take away all the hurt that Persephone gave you?"

"Careful nephew. You are my favorite of your brothers, but I am losing patience with this conversation."

This was why I liked the dead better.

Hephaestus shrugged. "Come and visit little Alkira," he said. "But be careful, she has a habit of pulling on beards. Cameron would like to see you too, I think." I harrumphed and walked away from my nephew into the maze of bookshelves. "I'll tell Cameron you're coming," Hephaestus shouted. There was a clatter and a happy chorus of barks as my nephew threw a giant bone for Cerberus before jogging up the marble stairs again.

He was right, I could admit that. I should visit my new niece. But everything else he'd said—ridiculous. I didn't need any of that. I didn't need a clingy mortal who demanded my attention and sent me on impossible errands to bring back exotic foods for their cravings as my brothers had done. They had done it willingly, eagerly... Zeus, Thunderer, standing in line for a triple caramel macchiato because Cameron had demanded something special from his favorite Brooklyn coffee shop—utterly ridiculous. Poseidon, lord of the seas, running through Olympus' marble halls with a seaweed salad.

I laughed loudly and the sound echoed through my empty library. This was where I belonged. With my books, my secrets, and my memories. That was what the dead were good for, and this was my domain.

I plucked the leather-wrapped book Gideon had given me from its place on the shelf and unwrapped it carefully. I had given it a cursory examination in the library, but my mind had been on other things. Now I could look closely as the work the young mortal had done. The stitching was intricate and well spaced in the new binding, and the paper he'd chosen for the inner cover complimented the deep wine red of the freshly repaired leather beautifully. He was skilled, that much was certain, but with Signore de Sarno as a mentor, he would have no choice.

I hadn't thought of claiming a mortal in centuries. Especially not since my brothers had been going through this fever to find the 'sparks' that had been scattered through the mortal world. I knew what the consequences of coupling with them meant. I would have to be careful.

When the curse was first discovered, Zeus had hammered down my door and demanded I bring him the shade of his lover so that he could be resurrected... but when I went down into the depths of my kingdom to do my brother's bidding, the young mortal's shade was nowhere to be found. Hera's curse was so complete that when the mortal died, she made sure that their soul was obliterated and that she could not be defeated.

I couldn't do that to Gideon... but I did want to possess him, claim him. I wanted to sink my teeth into the bruises I'd left on his throat. I threaded my way through the stacks of books to where Cerberus lay, gnawing on the ancient femur Hephaestus had thrown for him. "No one comes in," I said.

Cerberus growled happily and his tail whacked against my leg three times before I willed myself to earth—to Rome.

To Gideon.

I stood in the shadows, invisible to the mortals, watching them at their revels as I used to do in the old days. The thought brought a whisper of a smile to my face as I remembered the murmurs that had run through the crowd about 'death lurking in the shadows.' They were right, I was always watching. Not out of jealousy, but a perverse curiosity at how these mortals chose to spend the precious moments they had been given.

I hadn't expected to find Gideon in a place like this, a wine bar ablaze with light and stuffed with awkward-looking tourists and unwashed backpackers from all over the world. Gideon was sandwiched between two girls. The one with dark hair pushed glasses of beer towards him, but when she wasn't looking he gave them to whoever came near. *He was no fool, my librarian.*

I don't know how long I waited, but the crowd got progressively louder, and so did the music. Gideon had drunk the equivalent of one dark beer, and seemed to be looking for a way to escape the conversation he was having with the dark-haired girl. I thought I recognized her, but I couldn't be sure. Someone from the library, perhaps. And then she turned her head and peered into the shadows, her dark eyes searched the darkness as she stared right at me.

The shadows around me intensified, and the girl's eyes narrowed before she looked away and poured another glass of beer from the seemingly endless jug at her elbow. She hadn't touched a drop the entire time I'd been watching, but she seemed intent on getting Gideon drunk.

Where had I seen her before?

I concentrated on the pair and focused on their conversation.

"So, Gideon... tell me about that guy." The girl leaned in, tugging on his sleeve playfully.

"What? What guy?"

"You know what guy," she said. I watched as she slid closer to him and pushed a perspiring glass of dark beer into his hand. "The one with the tattoos... do you think he's tattooed everywhere?"

I grimaced and flexed my fingers.

Gideon laughed and pushed her hand away. "That's a silly question. And I still don't know what you're talking about."

"You know exactly who I'm talking about. Vittorio told me he's a patron of the library... very rich, very influential. Very sexy," she said with a wink.

"Uhhh... I guess," Gideon's voice sounded wary, and I felt a little sting of pleasure at his response.

"Don't be shy, Gideon, you can tell me."

"There's nothing to tell," he said.

That was a lie.

He took a quick sip of the beer and then pushed it away. The dark haired girl didn't seem to notice that someone else picked it up as they whirled by the table.

"Come on, Gid... Vittorio told me everything."

Gideon didn't flinch. "Oh, really?"

The young woman nodded. "Yup. He's seen you two talking... How did he describe it? Oh, yes... a heated argument. A lover's quarrel perhaps? You can tell me, Gideon. You know how much I love juicy gossip. A rich patron dallying with a lowly librarian? It's practically ripped straight out of a romance novel! Except, he's married and you're... well... you're you."

I watched Gideon shift in his seat. *Shit. She was playing hardball.* "What's that supposed to mean?"

"Don't take it personally," she said in a rush. "I just mean that it all sounds a little... ridiculous, don't you think?"

Gideon didn't answer, but the dark haired woman pressed on. "Has he said anything to you?"

"Said anything?" I saw his throat bob as he swallowed, hoping she wouldn't notice. "Like what?"

The girl shifted in her seat playfully. "I dunno... anything weird? Rich people are always so eccentric. He looks like the eccentric type, don't you think?"

Gideon shook his head. "Nope... sorry to disappoint you. Nothing weird. He's just a guy who likes books."

I couldn't take it any more. Her questions were becoming too personal; too pointed. I appeared out of nowhere, out of the shadows and closed my fingers around Gideon's arm. He looked up at me with wide, sober eyes, his expression one of surprise and the barest hint of arousal. "It's time to go," I growled.

"Gideon, aren't you going to introduce me to your friend?" the girl called out in surprise.

Insolent mortal. I drew myself up to my full height and glared down at her. The lights in the bar flickered ever so slightly, but she didn't move. There was a defiant curve to her lip and her eyes were as black and hard as lava rock.

Eris.

In an instant, the goddess was gone, and in her place was a bewildered looking girl with brown eyes who stared at me in surprise.

"Gideon, are you leaving?"

"Yeah, it's going to be a long night... I only meant to stop for one drink anyway. Signore Agesander needs to talk to me about some manuscripts he brought in... we're going to meet Signore de Sarno." He smiled and tugged on one of the girl's dark pigtails. "I'll see you tomorrow, Em," Gideon lied easily to the girl and I almost smiled.

"Sure... sounds good. Don't stay up too late. I'll see you in the morning!" The girl still looked confused as to how she had gotten there, and I wondered how long Eris had possessed her—and what she'd done before I'd arrived.

Gideon pulled his arm out of my grip and pulled his bag over his shoulder. "I guess I should thank you," he said somewhat begrudgingly.

"She asks a lot of questions."

"That's Emilie for you... she's not usually so nosey, but I guess we've been talking a lot more lately."

We walked casually for a few minutes and I allowed Gideon to lead the way. "I didn't come here to talk about books," I said finally, pausing at a corner. Gideon walked a few more paces and then stopped and turned to look at me. He was beautiful. The soft glow of the streetlamps played over the dark waves of his hair, and his eyes looked almost black. I wanted him, this mortal, and I could feel that he wanted me too. If I asked him, if I commanded him—

Gideon surprised me by closing the distance between us quickly, our chests almost touching. "I know," he said and before I could say anything, his arms were around my neck and he was reaching up to kiss me. With something more like a growl than a groan, I wrapped my arms around the mortal's waist and lifted him the rest of the way.

Our mouths crashed together, and I was stunned by how much I'd wanted this. Gideon's eyes were closed, and his lips were hot; insistent and hungry against mine. His tongue explored my mouth boldly, taking me by surprise again.

I leaned against the warm stones of the building behind me, enjoying the feel of Gideon's mouth on mine and the way his fingers curled tightly into my hair.

All at once, it hit me. Slow at first, like the first tendrils of smoke from a funeral pyre, and then in a rush of cold fire that thundered through my veins. I stiffened, unsure of what was happening.

Gideon's mouth opened under mine as I pulled him closer and he moaned deeply as my fingers dug into his hips. I could feel the growing hardness of his cock against me; he wanted me just as much as I wanted him.

Was this what my brothers had been talking about? Was this how they had known their spark from among all the others?

Gideon dragged his lips from mine and stared into my eyes. His pupils were wide and his gaze was full of lust. "Do you… want to see my apartment?" he asked quietly. He licked his lips, and I could almost hear his lascivious thoughts. He was remembering how I had dominated him in the library, and his cock pulsed against me as I held him easily with one arm. I reached up to trace a finger lightly over his jaw and trace the faint outlines of the bruises I'd gifted him with.

"Is that what you want?" I replied.

"Yes."

It was barely a whisper, and I pressed my lips to his firmly, knowing that my kiss held the promise of what I could do to him… it was everything he wanted.

"But you'll have to put me down," he said with a chuckle. He rubbed his thigh against my crotch and arched against me. "Otherwise we'll never get there."

I set him on his feet. "Don't get used to ordering me around," I said through gritted teeth.

"I'll take what I can get," he said with a cheeky smile.

Trouble.

. . .

We walked quickly through the Piazza Navona and I followed Gideon to a nondescript stone building and through a battered wooden door. He almost ran up a set of narrow stairs, pausing at each landing to make sure that I was following... higher, and higher, in the ancient building until we reached an even smaller staircase that led to Gideon's apartment. If it could even be called that. I raised an eyebrow as the door creaked open to reveal the loft space he called home. There was no bathroom that I could see, and one wall of the room was made entirely of windows. His bed was on a makeshift platform in front of them. Very bold indeed.

"A shared bathroom?" I commented blithely.

Gideon laughed as he walked to the small kitchen and pulled a bottle of wine and two mugs from the cupboard. "It's not ideal, but it's cheap, and the *Vallicelliana* covers some of it... I wouldn't want to be too much farther from the library. I spend most of my time there."

He pulled out the cork with a practiced motion and poured the wine into the mugs with a smile on his face. He picked one up, leaving the other on the narrow kitchen counter for me to retrieve.

"Besides... unless you're a pigeon, this is the best view in the city." Gideon unlocked one of the tall windows beside his bed and stepped out onto a tiny balcony that looked as though it was hanging on to the side of the building by a thread. *He was fearless, this librarian. Or maybe just stupid.* He stood there, staring out across the Piazza Navona with a contemplative look on his handsome face, waiting for me.

Even though the sun had set, the Piazza was still bustling. I imagined what it would look like in the daytime, crowded with tourists snapping pictures and buying useless souvenirs, trivializing the ancient city's beauty for the sake of a few Facebook likes. They would go home and tell their friends how lovely it was here, how romantic— but in reality, they had barely seen the city at all, except through a camera's lens. And when their fleeting lives had passed and they tried to look back on these precious moments where they believed they'd been happiest, they would realize that they had never truly lived them at all, and would weep bitter tears at their loss. I'd seen it before, a hundred thousand times over. *Mortals were all the same.* And their afterlife would be no different…

But Gideon… Gideon saw the world for what it was, because he took the time to really look.

Perhaps that was why he'd seen me, *pursued me*, even before I could see him for what he truly was.

I took the mug of wine that he'd poured me and sniffed at it delicately before taking a sip. I grimaced at the taste. It was worth every cent of the two euros it had been purchased with. I stood in his pathetic excuse for a kitchen and admired the sharp silhouette Gideon's body cut against the velvety darkness. He didn't look up as I stepped out onto the balcony with him; his eyes were fixed on the dome of St. Peter's Basilica in the distance.

"There are a hundred and forty statues of saints in the basilica," he said, gesturing toward it with his mug. "That's a whole lot of virtue under one roof."

I took a disinterested sip of my wine. "I've never been much for virtue. Vices are more fun. This is terrible."

Gideon shrugged and drank from his own mug and made a face. He tapped his fingers against the ancient railing of the balcony. "Which are your favorite?" he asked after a moment.

"Oh, a little of this, a little of that. I could show you if you like."

Finally, he turned to look at me, and I could see the desire in his eyes. But his brows were curved in a sardonic frown.

"Just to be clear… we're going to have to have some boundaries. I'm not going to be some kind of pet. I work at the library, you're a patron… you can't just do that whenever you like."

"Oh, no?" I asked with a cold smile, enjoying the way he shivered at the change in my expression. "You seemed to enjoy our last interlude. You spilled all over yourself like a schoolboy catching his first glimpse of his crush's underpants."

He took a step toward me. I stood my ground, and took another casual sip from my mug and observed him coolly.

"I won't deny that I like it a little… rough," he said, his jaw twitching at the admission. "But that doesn't mean I'll beg."

"I had you begging before," I reminded him.

"Yeah, and you showed me just how far that'll get me with you," he countered.

"It wasn't the right time," I said graciously. "But I'm willing to reevaluate."

"Oh, how thoughtful of you. I suppose you want me to get down on my knees and suck you off right here... Right now."

"The thought had crossed my mind."

He wet his lips. "Fine. But only because I want to."

I put one hand on his head and brushed my fingers through his dark curls before pushing him down onto his knees. "Works for me."

He reached to unbutton my pants; I helped him by stepping out of them as he slipped them down my legs. He mouthed at my cock through my briefs before removing those as well. I reached for my wine and drank deeply as he took me in his mouth, still soft but quickly filling out as he licked and sucked. My fingers stroked through his hair—then I snatched a handful of it and yanked him back so he could look up at me with those hungry eyes.

"You like it rough?"

"Yes," he said, through clenched teeth.

"Good," I breathed, and pushed him back onto my cock, forcing him to take me deeper than before.

He gagged almost at once, and I let him draw back and take a breath before pushing into his mouth again. His hands came up to clutch at my thighs—not to shove me away, but just for something to hold on to—his nails dug into my flesh almost deep enough to draw blood and I stiffened as that same cold fire rushed through me once more. I cradled his skull, directing him as I pleased, forcing him to swallow down another inch of my cock even as the tears rose in his eyes and drool spilled down his chin and onto the tile below.

He gagged again and almost choked, and I made a small sound of pity, holding him in place as he tried to draw back.

"Careful now, librarian. Relax," I said softly.

He blinked, the first tears running down his cheeks—but he did as he was told, and eventually I pulled my cock out of his mouth and let him savor a gasping breath of air.

I continued to use his mouth roughly for several minutes, looking out across the view of the Piazza as I finished my wine and enjoyed the obscene, wet sounds Gideon was making against the backdrop of the city's nighttime hum. The cold fire coursed dully through my veins, and the tendrils of smoke began to wind themselves around my brain. When my mug was empty, I set it down on the railing and let go of his hair.

He drew back to catch his breath, and wiped the saliva from his chin before massaging his jaw.

"Go inside and get naked," I commanded.

He huffed out a laugh. "You can't boss me around my own apartment."

"Can't I?"

Gideon climbed to his feet and stepped towards me, his hand dropping to stroke my cock, but I caught his wrist before he had the chance.

"Would you prefer I bent you over your kitchen counter and fucked you so hard that your screaming would make your neighbors call the police?" I breathed.

He fixed me with a cynical little smile. "If you say please. We are civilized men after all, are we not?" He raised an eyebrow. "Well, at least one of us is... I'm not so sure about you."

My grip on his wrist tightened, but I knew when to pick my battles with this one—and I didn't want to invite further discussion about my true nature. "Please."

I released him, and he turned and ducked back into his apartment, stripping off his shirt as he went.

"You ought to say please more often," he called back over his shoulder. "My mother always said you'll catch more flies with honey than vinegar."

"What I ought to do is put you over my knee," I muttered, following him back inside. By the time I stepped through the window and latched it tightly, he was fully nude, and lounging on his bed.

"Get on your hands and knees," I said.

He raised an eyebrow. "What part of I'm not going to be your pet did you not understand?"

"Do you want me to give you pleasure or not?"

Gideon frowned just a little. "Why can't I be on my back? I'd like to look at you."

"Because if you're on your hands and knees, it will be easier for me to spank you until you reconsider your infernal petulance."

He bit his lip. "That actually sounds pretty good." He crawled up onto the comforter and got into position. "There are condoms the top drawer of the dresser. The lube's in there, too. You're bigger than I'm used to. My jaw's going to ache for days."

"All business, librarian," I said with a smirk.

"Practical..." he replied somewhat defensively.

I yanked open the top drawer of his rickety dresser. The lube was nestled amongst his neatly folded underwear along with a half-empty packet of condoms. I ripped the wrapper off one with my teeth and rolled it over my cock, still hard with anticipation and the muted fire that rippled through my limbs.

Even if he hadn't suggested protection, I would have helped myself. I had to be careful; I was still unsure about everything. Including the prophecy. I gritted my teeth and grabbed the lube as I climbed onto the bed.

"Who folds their damn underwear?" I muttered as I stroked the lube over my member. He squirmed as I poured more of the cold fluid down his ass and teased at his hole with my thumb. He was ready for me... eager. And he would get what he wanted. Soon enough.

"I'm sure the customs are quite different where you're from," he said, a teasing note in his voice. "Where's that again? I don't think I've asked you that before... Signore de Sarno doesn't seem to know either..."

Gideon gasped as I cut off any further discussion on the topic by pushing one long finger into him as far as the second knuckle. He arched his back, adjusting to the sudden intrusion.

"Jesus, give me some warning next time!"

I ignored him and worked a second finger in impatiently, twisting and curling them, getting him ready for me. When he opened his mouth to say something else, I smacked his ass with the other hand, hard enough to leave a vivid red brand against his pale flesh.

"Fuuuuck," he hissed, hanging his head, his hair falling over his eyes. "You're a goddamn sadist, you know that?"

I answered with another slap, against his sensitive inner thigh this time. I watched his legs tremble with the effort of staying still. My fingers were still moving inside him, rubbing none too delicately against that sweet spot deep inside, and he was soon struggling to bite back his whimpers as I pushed another finger into his hole and fucked him swiftly with them. When I finally pulled them out, he let out a breathless moan and buried his face in the crook of his elbow.

"Don't be gentle," he said; his words were muffled but unmistakable.

I let a satisfied smile that he couldn't see play over my lips. "I had no intention of being."

I lined myself up behind Gideon and entered him, giving him just a moment to adjust to the sensation, and my girth, before pressing all the way in—one long, smooth stroke that knocked the breath out of him. I saw his hands grip the comforter tightly; heard the breathy groan that left his chest. Drawing almost all the way out, I slammed back into him with enough force to drive him into the mattress.

My fingers gripped his hips tightly, delighting in digging fresh bruises into that exquisite canvas before the marks around his throat had fully faded—and knowing, despite his protestations, that he'd wear them in secret like a badge of honor.

He'd touch them when he was alone, digging his own fingers into them in a vain attempt to feel what he felt now, this sublime surrender, this ecstasy at giving himself to me.

That cold fire was muted, but still rippled in the background, begging to be set free; I could feel it with every thrust. Below me, Gideon bit his forearm hard enough to draw blood as I drove into him again and again. His whimpers gave way to gasping cries as my strokes grazed that sensitive spot deep inside him; his cock, hanging hard and heavy between his legs, leaked a steady stream of precum onto the bed. I doubt he even noticed.

From his lips tumbled a desperate invocation, a babbled orison of "harder," "more," and "please!" I had a reputation for turning a deaf ear to prayers, but how could I now, with such a fine offering laid before me? I obliged him, pushing his body until I'm sure he felt he was reaching his breaking point. And as I looked down upon this willing sacrifice, this honey-sweet libation poured out beneath me, I felt myself loving him helplessly—and on the tails of that love, a tempestuous desire to tear him apart.

All at once, I had to know; I had to know if that cold fire would consume me if I gave in to my curiosity. If I was wrong, he would be gone forever. But if I was right, if the oracle had not lied...

He was too far gone in pleasure to notice when I pulled out and tore the condom from my cock and tossed it to the floor. I stared down at his beautiful, writhing form. He looked so mortal. So breakable.

But if he was the one...

I entered him then, bare, before my foolish hopes could creep into my mind. Gideon was so open for me now, so slick, that it felt like his body had been molded perfectly to fit mine. As soon as I thrust into him, that same cold fire that had only rippled in the shadows of my mind ripped through my veins and I groaned in ecstasy as my limbs shuddered with it.

Gideon moaned as I picked up my pace again, and soon he was gasping that his orgasm was close. I struggled to regain control of my faculties, and since I'd recklessly thrown him into mortal danger without his knowledge, I decided, for a change, to show mercy.

I leaned forward and wrapped one hand around his cock, smoothing the other down his trembling back; I began to stroke him in time with my powerful thrusts. This beautiful man, this mortal, he was waiting for my permission—whether he realized or not—I gave it.

"Cum for me," I whispered.

He did, and with a deep groan I watched his climax ripple through him. His semen striped the comforter in copious ribbons just moments before he collapsed onto them, boneless. I did not give him time to recover, and braced one foot against his shoulder for better leverage as I fucked him hard and fast. That cold fire rolled over and through me, consuming me like nothing I'd ever experienced before. It was heady and intoxicating. Ethereal. Gideon was too exhausted to help, merely moaning as I came deep inside him.

"Asshole, I told you to use a condom," he mumbled as I strode to the kitchen to clean myself up in the small metal sink. I ignored him. My heart was racing, my limbs vibrating with sensations I had never experienced before.

My lover slumped on the bed, but he wasn't dead.

I supposed I should have been relieved, but I wasn't.

I was terrified.

When I turned back to Gideon, I saw that he'd managed to roll onto his back, but sitting up still seemed beyond him. I could see smears of his semen on his chest where he'd laid on it. And my own divine seed was still inside him…

I crossed over to the bed and stretched out beside him. I ran my fingers through his hair and then gathered him against my chest, unsure if I was trying to comfort him or myself. My expression was unreadable, but my mind was reeling.

It was him… my spark. Any doubts I'd had before seemed absurd now in the bright light of the afterglow. I felt as though a veil had been lifted from my eyes; I was seeing Gideon clearly for the first time, and the truth was blinding.

"That was the best orgasm I've ever had in my life," he murmured, reaching up to catch my fingers in his own. He squeezed them gently and rested his head against my shoulder, his body fitted perfectly against mine. "It really does feel like you die a little… doesn't it?" he said softly. "But I'm sure you know all about death."

I snatched my hand away. My skin prickled where he touched me. The sensation was almost unbearable in its intensity. *What was I doing?*

In a second, I was on my feet and striding for the door. Gideon struggled to sit up and grimaced from some bruise or other I'd given him.

"Where are you going?" His voice was strangled and confused, and I couldn't meet his eyes.

"Away," I said shortly. "Don't look for me."

"What the fuck?" he cried. "Your pants are on the balcony!"

Before he could say anything, I pulled the shadows forward to envelop me and willed myself back to Olympus. I couldn't bear the touch of his skin any longer or the way I felt when I was around him. It was too real, too mortal. And if the way my own body had betrayed me was any indication, I did not know what I could trust anymore.

I needed time, and that was one luxury I didn't have.

CHAPTER 10 ~ GIDEON

I've been ghosted before… but never literally.

I sat there on the bed, my body shaking with the aftermath of the best sex of my life, and stared in disbelief at the empty corner of my apartment where Aiden had just stood. It wasn't a figment of my imagination; it wasn't some trick of my sex-addled brain. He'd disappeared. He didn't open the door, I didn't hear his heavy steps on the stairs… and his goddamned jeans were still on my tiny balcony.

"Fucking hell," I muttered as I flopped back on my ruined bed and pulled a pillow over my face to yell into it. I barely knew how to rationalize what had happened—the sex alone was enough to make any sane person's head spin. Aiden had known exactly what I wanted, and given it to me without any hesitation. I'd never felt so dirty, or so adored as I did when he was fucking me. Each stroke had brought a new sensation crashing down on my body, and I could still feel the cold fire of my orgasm pulsing in my veins.

That was a new one. I'd had plenty of orgasms, and good ones, but nothing I'd ever experienced compared to that. Not by a long shot.

I groaned and rolled over. I knew I should go take a shower, but I really didn't want to move any further than this bed. All I really wanted was to fall asleep against Aiden's chest, but instead, all I could do was grab my pillow and try to forget about him.

Fat chance.

For the first time ever, I slept through my alarm. *Like the dead.* The warm sunshine on my face was the only thing that ripped me from my dream. It was probably a good thing. I'd been wandering through a dark library, trailing my fingers along the spines of the leatherbound books that surrounded me. *Don't look for me.* The last words Aiden had said before he'd fucking disappeared into shadows had echoed in my ears as I walked between the stacks. The marble floor was cold under my bare feet and my eyes were trying desperately to adjust to the darkness. *Don't look for me.* A candle flared to life in a stone alcove and I rushed towards it, but before my fingers could close around the wax pillar, a door opened. The light that spilled through blinded me and startled me enough to wake me up. *Late. So late.* I was usually up early enough to watch the sun rise over the city… not today.

Don't look for me.

"No problem, asshole," I muttered as I pulled myself out of bed and tried to shake off the dream. I was no stranger to pain… but this morning, everything hurt. I gritted my teeth as I rushed through my shower. Aiden had definitely left his mark on me, and I had the bruises to prove it. I smiled just a little as I pressed my fingers into one of the dark prints on my hip. His fingers had been there, holding on in a death grip while he'd fucked me. A delicious shiver ran up my spine and something cold flared in my chest. I pulled up my jeans and tried not to wince as they rubbed over the marks.

"You're being stupid. It was just a one-time thing," I muttered as I threw my discarded clothes from the night before onto my bed. I was overdue for a trip to the laundromat anyway. I retrieved Aiden's jeans and underwear from the balcony and used them to pick up the condom he'd thrown on the floor last night. I must have slammed the window a little harder than I should have because a stream of Italian curses and thumping on the floor erupted from the apartment below. Ordinarily I would have smiled, but I wasn't in the mood. I stomped hard on the floor on my way to the kitchen and shoved Aiden's clothes and the condom into the garbage can.

"Fuck you," I muttered.

Another *thump* from below. "And fuck you!" I shouted. "*Cazzo! Vaffanculo!*" I stomped harder and grabbed my bag. I ran down the stairs to the street and didn't stop running until I reached the *Vallicelliana*.

I tried to creep in with a group of tourists, but Emilie saw me and a catlike smile spread over her face. "You can't hide from me, Gideon Vogel... I expect a *full* report!"

I ducked my head and made a beeline for the archive room. Signore de Sarno would be waiting to give me an earful for being late. Maybe I could lie to him... say that I was speaking to the owner of the books. I mean, we hadn't done much talking... but it wasn't entirely a lie either.

The archive room door was closed, and I prepared myself for the stream of invective that would greet me when I opened it. But the handle didn't turn.

"Locked? But I'm so late..."

"Sooooo...." Emilie sidled up to me as I fished for my keys. She leaned against the wall and crossed her arms over her chest and fixed her dark eyes on me. "You left the bar with that guy... the guy who comes into the library all the time. He looked way taller than I remember. Is he tattooed all the way? You can tell me." She poked me in the ribs playfully and I winced.

"Knock it off."

"Rough night, huh? Are you hungover? I mean, I won't tell Signore de Sarno if you are, I was feeling a little shitty myself this morning... I still have a headache."

I groaned as I realized I'd left my keys on the kitchen counter. I'd definitely had my mind elsewhere... *Stupid. So stupid.*

"What?"

"I left my keys at home. Where is Signore de Sarno?"

Emilie shook her head. "You're in luck, he'll be in meetings all day. Up on the mezzanine. I'm supposed to order in lunch for him."

"Meetings? Really?"

Emilie smiled. "Yup… with your new boyfriend."

"Shut up," I muttered. "It's not like that."

"Oh, isn't it?" She wiggled her eyebrows and I glared down at her. "Fine, fine, if that's the way you want to be about it. I was going to ask you to help me deliver it, but I won't now."

"Good. I don't want to see him."

That was only half true, I did want to see him. So I could yell at him for being such an asshole.

"Riiiight." Emilie stared at me until I jiggled the locked door handle again.

"If you're done interrogating me, I'd like to get to work now," I said tersely.

"I'm not done," she said, "but I have to order the Signore's lunch. You need to lighten up, Gid. It's not a big deal."

"Whatever, just get me the keys. And *don't* tell me to lighten up."

Emilie shrugged and skipped back to the desk to retrieve the master keys. She pulled the archive room set off the ring and flung them down the hallway at me as another group of tourists came in.

I caught them awkwardly and let myself into the archive room with a sigh of relief. It didn't look like Signore de Sarno had even been in here today. So much the better. I closed the door and flipped on as few lights as possible. If everyone left me alone for the rest of the day, I might be able to make it through. But just barely.

Even though it galled me just a little to work on Aiden's books every day, at least I didn't have to look at him. Signore de Sarno only mentioned him if I asked questions, and I was doing my best not to ask. It was easy to zone out while I was working, but I was trying my best to stay as focused as possible.

When I stopped focusing, my mind would drift to him… and his image would float into my brain like smoke. Hazy at first, and then stronger as each memory etched itself into my subconscious. The curve of the dragons that were tattooed on his chest and arms, the way his long fingers had traced their way down my spine, the sound of his groan as he came, and that cold fire that flared in my chest every time I thought about him. It was intoxicating, and too easy to give in. It had been one night.

And I was a wreck about it.

Two weeks had passed, and Signore de Sarno had collected the manuscripts as I completed them—no doubt to return them to their master—without any comment beyond the usual words of praise for my work or some small suggestion to improve the next manuscript.

I'd been feeling strangely exhausted lately, and no matter how early I went to bed or how late I slept on the weekends, I couldn't seem to catch up. My dreams had gotten weird too. I was always in a dark library; always looking for something I couldn't find—something just out of reach—not a book, but a person. But I couldn't even be sure if it was a person, or if I was just chasing shadows.

Whatever it was, I would never wake up feeling rested and it was starting to show.

"Gideon… you've been shelving that same trolley of books for the last two hours." Emilie's voice jolted me out of whatever trance I was in and I rubbed my eyes before looking at her.

"I'm sorry, what?"

"Didn't you hear me calling you? I must have been shushed a million times between here and the front desk." Emilie pointed at a few of the older patrons accusingly, but they ignored her. All they wanted was quiet, and I didn't blame them. My head pounded with a sudden headache and I leaned on the trolley.

"No, I didn't hear you. What do you want?"

"It's not me, it's Signore de Sarno. He wanted you to take this to Mr. Agggy… Aggehs—" Emilie hesitated, struggling with the name.

"Agesander, sure."

Emilie shrugged and shoved a heavy book wrapped in a familiar piece of soft leather into my chest. "Great. Here you go."

I grabbed it quickly and cradled it in my arms. "Can't you do it?"

"No way, that guy freaks me out. He's all yours!" Before I could protest, Emilie was headed back for the front desk; her black hair swung across her shoulders like a live thing and I suddenly felt nauseous.

"Fine," I muttered and shifted the book in my arms. It would take five seconds and then I could get back to work. I'd just hand it to him and be done with it. *At least, that's what I told myself I'd do.*

I checked the stacks quickly to be sure he wasn't on the main floor before heaving a sigh and climbing the spiral stairs that led to the mezzanine. My cheeks burned as I remembered how he had dominated me on these stairs, his long tattooed fingers tight around my throat as I had gasped out my climax.

"Asshole," I muttered.

"Talking to yourself again, librarian," a coldly bored voice said from above me. I looked up and gritted my teeth as Aiden's pale eyes burned into mine.

"I'm looking for you," I huffed as I mounted the last of the stairs and stepped onto the mezzanine. I held the book out for him. "Here. Take it."

He took it from me and I bit my lip hard to keep from shouting at him. *How dare he just leave me like that... how dare he not contact me... how dar—*

Instead of speaking, I turned and reached for the railing of the spiral staircase.

"Going so soon, librarian," he said lazily.

That was it.

I spun to face him, my face red with anger.

"You're an asshole, you know that? No, don't answer that. I'm sure you know," I spat. It was hard to keep my voice low, and even harder to keep it from shaking. "Who the hell do you think you are? Do you really think you can treat me like that… fuck me like that... and then pretend as though nothing happened?" I stared at him, cheeks blazing and my heart thundering in my chest. I'd never been this angry in my entire life, and Aiden, that bastard, he just watched me with an amused expression in his shockingly pale eyes.

"Well?"

"Well, what? I told you not to look for me. What happened doesn't mean anything. We used each other, don't you agree?"

He was infuriatingly calm and I wanted to throw things at his expressionless face. "No, goddamnit, I don't fucking agree!"

"Language… we're in a library, Gideon," he said smoothly as he unwrapped the book and ran his fingers over the newly repaired cover that I'd spent hours rubbing with beeswax. I wanted to slap it out of his hands and kick it over the railing onto the floor below.

"Look. I didn't ask you for anything, I get it. You didn't promise me anything. I get it. But you at least owe me some fucking courtesy."

Aiden ignored me and brought the book to his nose to inhale the smell of the parchment, leather, and wax and I ground my teeth as he stayed silent. *Asshole.*

"If it meant nothing to you, it won't be hard for you to stay away," I said shortly. "You're a patron of the library, whatever, but you don't need to speak to me, and you don't need to ask for me, ever."

He still didn't reply, and I stared at him, furious. I'd be waiting forever. Without thinking, I pushed the book aside and wrapped my arm around his neck. With a quick motion I pulled his face down to my height to kiss him. The moment our lips touched, that cold fire that had been slowly spinning in my chest pulsed and crashed through my veins. Aiden stiffened for just a moment, and I put every ounce of anger and passion I was holding back into that kiss. If he could tell me that it hadn't meant anything after that, then I'd be done.

When I finally broke the kiss and released him, we were both breathing fast and I could see the unmistakable outline of his arousal against the front of his dark jeans. Identical to the ones I'd thrown in the trash the morning after he'd abandoned me. His pale eyes swirled with something I couldn't explain and I brushed a hand over my lips.

I'd never felt this way about anyone... and the physical reaction I had to him was impossible to deny. But if I had to, I would.

"Well?"

But Aiden was silent as he straightened up and ran a hand over his perfectly neat hair. I let out a furious breath and turned on my heel once more, intent on escaping his presence as quickly as I could so I didn't have to think about how it felt to be around him.

I paused with my foot on the top stair and my hand on the railing and turned to face him again. "You need to know something," I said briskly. "I know you don't belong here... I think I've always known. There's something shady about you... something not quite right. That's what makes all of this so much worse."

"Oh, really?" was his only reply.

I should have stopped talking, but I couldn't stop now.

"Signore de Sarno told me about your family... how there's been an Agesander present at the *Vallicelliana* since its formation... I refuse to believe that's true. I looked you up. I looked up your family—they don't exist. You don't exist."

Aiden's face had grown darker as I spoke, but I didn't care about that either. I just had to get it out and I couldn't stop myself. "Sure, your name is in the archives, but it's nowhere else. Not in the census, not in the phone book... nowhere. How do you expect me to believe that you're some wealthy patron with no paper trail, no charitable works, no fucking address?" My voice had risen just a little, drawing the attention of a few patrons, but I didn't care. "And when I Googled you... do you know what comes up? Do you even know? A mythology lesson. That's what." I stared at him boldly. "Who the fuck are you?" I challenged him.

He was only silent for a moment, and then I realized how close he was to me. "Do you really want to know, librarian?"

I lifted my chin and stood my ground. The spiral staircase yawned behind me.

"Yes. I think you owe me the truth."

"Do I now?" he asked; his voice was dangerously quiet and I began to feel a little nervous. I took a breath to say something, but my words were cut off as his pale fingers wrapped around my throat. He lifted me into the air with ease, bringing my face level with his. My feet kicked the empty air and I clawed at his hand and forearm, trying desperately to make him release me.

"You mortals… so arrogant in your assertions," he hissed in my ear. "You think you can cheat death, gain immortality through these vain pursuits. All I see, covering every wall, is the pathetic attempt to scratch some kind of permanence from this gift you've been given… this gift that you squander in meaningless scurrying. In the end, you all come to me. In the end, the bitter taste on your tongue will not be regret, it will be the coin that paid your fare across the Acheron." His grip eased just a little, allowing me to draw the barest hint of a breath.

He stared into my eyes, the pale blue clouding even further as his pupils widened like black whirlpools. The longer I stared, the darker they became, pools of oil filled with writhing bodies, their mouths stretched in silent screams of agony.

"Please," I managed to whisper.

"Yes… that's what I want to hear librarian, I want to hear you beg… beg for your life. In this life, or the one that comes after, you will be mine, and your shade will be my pet to use as I wish… you are in no position to demand anything from me."

I struggled weakly, gasping for air, as he smiled at me coldly and pressed his cruel lips to mine. That cold fire surged inside me once more and I heard his gasp of surprise before his grip loosened and I fell to the mezzanine floor, my chest heaving and my breaths ragged and painful as the air rushed back into my screaming lungs.

The library was silent except for the creaking of the wooden floor below, and I grasped the railing tightly to drag myself to my feet. Tendrils of black mist curled along the floor, spilled over and down the spiral stairs, and wound their way up my legs. But Aiden… or whatever his name was… was gone.

I slumped against the railing, breathing hard as I tried to make sense of what had happened. It was too much to believe.

Impossible. Utterly impossible.

Maybe I *was* losing my mind.

CHAPTER 11 ~ HADES

Who do you think you are?

He had dared me to show myself. That insolent mortal had dared to stand there and call me a liar.

"A liar!" I shouted and flung my goblet of wine across the room. The black glass shattered against the marble stones and blood red wine dripped down to the floor. Cerberus bent his heads to inspect the dark puddle and then yelped and skittered away as I hurled a golden plate with the same violence as the cup that had preceded it. Purple grapes bounced and rolled along the floor and I crushed one under my heel.

How dare he.

How dare he challenge me. This librarian... this mortal... this...

A pewter bowl filled with dark red pomegranates caught my eye and I lifted one and examine it carefully before crushing it in my fist. The tart juice ran down my arm and dripped onto the floor to stain my bare feet, but I didn't care. The ruined fruit splashed into the puddle of wine as I threw it away with a disgusted sneer.

I ripped tapestries from the wall, smashed ancient jars, and dented golden plates. With each item I destroyed, Gideon's face was burned deeper into my memories. The way he had spoken to me in the library just now—full of fire and conviction—this was what I craved; my own secret desire.

I didn't want a docile partner. I'd had a pale, silent consort for centuries, and look where that had gotten me. I ground the pomegranate into the marble stones and gritted my teeth. I needed a challenge, and somewhere, whatever Fate had aligned me with Gideon had known...

I clenched my hands in anger, looking for something else to throw and found nothing but my books.

There was no denying what I had felt. No way to avoid it. But how could I go to him now? How could I tell him that he had been right all along? He would throw it in my face, that's how it would go.

I paced the library while my mind whirled, replaying every moment we had shared, analyzing every word spoken—how had I not known sooner? How had I been so blind to his true nature, *and why was I now trying so hard to escape it?*

But *he* had pursued *me*—something had pulled him to me. *Were the Fates on our side after all?*

In a fit of frustration, I pushed over a stack of books and roared in anger as they toppled to the floor. Wine soaked into their ancient pages and I cursed myself for being so blind to the truth. I had been so busy avoiding the prophecy that I had ruined my chance at fulfilling it. If I went to Gideon now he would laugh.

The God of Death—afraid of an apology. *How ridiculous.* I deserved Gideon's laughter.

"What did you do now, brother?"

Zeus.

I grabbed the flagon of wine and drank deeply before throwing it against the wall with a *crash*.

A baby's startled cry cut through the noise and I froze as my brother came down the stairs and into the library holding his newborn goddess in his arms. She was wrapped in a snowy white woolen blanket shot through with gold threads, no doubt woven by Pan from wool taken from his personal flocks.

Cerberus barked happily at the intrusion and bounced around the pair like a puppy; his tail wagged crazily and knocked more items I hadn't already broken onto the floor before I shooed him away.

"Hush now," Zeus crooned to the infant. "Uncle Hades has a nasty temper, does he not? You shall have to teach him patience my little flower."

The baby gurgled in reply and reached up to grip her father's finger tightly. Zeus' beatific smile made my stomach churn. He came closer and held the child out to me.

"I'm not hungry," I snapped, waving the baby away.

"I will forgive your absence this time… but you can't avoid this any longer. You haven't been properly introduced to your niece," Zeus said firmly. "Take her."

"This isn't a good time," I said through gritted teeth. My brother's gaze tracked over the destruction in my library, and I watched an amused expression spread over his face.

"This is the perfect time." He held the baby out to me again. I glowered at my brother but this time I took the child. I held her awkwardly at first, and then settled her against my chest.

"Alkira, Goddess of the Spring Winds, meet your uncle… Hades *Polyxenos*, Lord of the Dark Kingdom of the Underworld," Zeus said solemnly. The child moved gently in my arms and blinked up at me with wide violet eyes. Her bloodline was clear, this descendant of two gods—ancient and modern.

"I don't recall any of your children being so… small." I said after a moment. "Or having so many freckles." I tapped the child's tiny nose with one long finger.

At my words, a light breeze that smelled of rain-wet grass and wildflowers blew through the library.

"She gets her freckles from Cameron," Zeus said softly. "And I think she likes you."

"No one likes me," I replied grimly. I looked down at the little goddess' face as she burbled up at me and reached to tug at my beard.

"Then you had best treasure any ally that crosses your path, no matter how small."

He wasn't wrong, but he didn't need to know that. My younger brother had a habit of being a smug bastard when it suited him—and it always suited him.

"I hope you'll visit the nursery more often," he said casually. I disentangled my new niece's fingers from my beard and handed her back to her father.

"We shall see. I've been busy."

"I've noticed," Zeus snapped as he shifted his daughter in his arms while she fussed and reached for me. "We've all noticed. For someone claiming not to be touched by the prophecy, you are spending an inordinate amount of time on earth."

"Perhaps I am," I replied as casually as I could. "You said yourself that we should be searching in earnest for our sparks—"

Zeus' laughter cut my words short and I glared at him as he doubled over with mirth. "You cannot be serious," he cried. "My dear, gloomy brother, next in line to find the mortal destined to bear his children? Forgive me, but I cannot—" The ruler of Olympus stomped on the marble floor as his laughter overcame him once more.

"Save your breath," I snapped.

While Zeus wiped at his tears, quieted his squalling daughter, and struggled to bring his laughter under control, I crossed my arms over my chest and glared at him.

"Ah, brother, I am sorry. Truly. But you must see the humor in it. Death himself brought low by a mortal... it cannot be so."

"When you put it like that it sounds even worse," I muttered.

"What happened?"

"I lied to him."

Now it was my brother's turn to stare. "One rule for you and another for the rest? I don't know why I expected more from you, Hades."

"Save your lectures," I snapped. "What's done is done, he would never have me now."

"Are you so sure?"

"What does it matter..."

"But you claimed him... you took him and felt everything Poseidon and I have described?"

I didn't have to answer; he already knew he was right. All at once, Zeus' expression changed. "How could you neglect your own warning?" he shouted at me. His eyes blazed with fury as he rounded on me. "You have left him vulnerable, this mortal. You have abandoned your spark to the goddess' wrath—how could you be so selfish?"

At my brother's words, I finally shook myself out of the angry trance I'd been consumed by. Gideon was my responsibility now. Whether he hated me or not, I had put him in danger.

"Eris."

"What? What did you say?"

"Eris," I repeated myself. The pieces were finally falling into place; I'd just been too blinded to see them. "She was there. She possessed a girl who volunteers at the *Vallicelliana*. I saw her and she fled."

"What?" Zeus roared.

"The library, *my* library—" I stopped mid-shout as a rush of premonition snaked its way up my spine. Alkira's terrified wail filled the air and Cerberus howled along with her until Zeus quieted them both.

In the blink of an eye, I was standing by my black basalt throne, staring down into the cistern that acted as our window into the mortal world. Zeus appeared a moment later, the child deposited back with Cameron in the nursery.

"Gideon," I whispered, trying in vain to see him through the fog that was presented to me. "Why can't I see him?"

"Father!" Hermes arrived on Olympus with a howling wind at his heels. Our messenger always traveled with haste, but his expression was filled with worry, something I'd never seen in him before.

"What is it?" I bellowed. I strode to my nephew and grabbed him by the edge of his tunic to draw him close to my face. "What news?"

Hermes gulped as the chill of my grip seeped into his skin, but Zeus intervened to push me away. "Calm, brother," he snapped.

"It's the library... the *Vallicelliana*. There's been an earthquake—"

My roar of anger filled the marble hall, and before my nephew could finish his sentence, I was gone.

CHAPTER 12 ~ GIDEON

After whatever the fuck had happened between Aiden and I, I'd left the library and hid out in my apartment. Alternately angry and upset while I scolded myself for being so fucking stupid. I couldn't even rationalize what I'd seen. There was only one explanation, but it was the most ridiculous thing I could ever have imagined.

Myths were lies. Stories made up by a society who couldn't explain what was happening to their world or their emotions. How do you explain loving someone you were never meant to love? Eros did it with his barbed shafts. Easy to blame your actions on an invisible deity. It happened every day in the modern world, but somehow it was more acceptable when couched in Christian terms.

The gods belonged in the fiction section of the library. End of story. Aiden was just… he was… "Goddamnit, Gideon, he disappeared into thin air in front of you… twice!" My shout echoed in my tiny apartment. There was a *thump* from the floor below me and I resisted the urge to jump up and down. I settled for stomping the length of the apartment, fuming the entire time. Who the hell did he think he was, and what the hell was with all that creepy shit he'd said? Unbelievable. *Un.* Believable. Was he trying to scare me with that hocus pocus act? It hadn't worked. If anything, it just made me sad that he had chosen to shroud his life in such ridiculous lies. *Did he really believe them? Did he really think he was some kind of god?*

A week passed. And then another, and Aiden still didn't have the balls to show his face in the library. I'd be lying if I said I wasn't looking for him. I even followed a guy walking a black dog for three blocks before I realized it wasn't him. I didn't even know what I'd do if I found him. *Something stupid, no doubt about that.*

With each day that passed I thought I'd be able to forget about him, but it was entirely the opposite, and every night I dreamed about the cold, dark library. That heavy exhaustion I'd tried to explain away as stress hadn't gone away either, but I had work to do, and it was the best way to forget about him—at least, that's what I kept telling myself.

On a day just like the others, I was awake before my alarm, but it was a struggle to get out of bed. I thought I'd eaten some bad risotto, or maybe I was coming down with something, but whatever it was, I felt like shit. I was tired all the time, and even the slightest whiff of cooking meat made my stomach turn over. I've never thrown up in public; it's a personal point of pride. But I almost did it three times on the way to the *Vallicelliana* that morning.

Emilie wasn't her usual chipper self that morning, either, and she returned my half-hearted greeting with an unexpectedly lukewarm response.

"You look like shit," I said, knowing that I looked about the same.

"Thanks. Most people just say something like, 'you look tired,'" she said with a wan smile.

"Yeah, well, I'm not a very good liar," I replied. "What's your excuse? I think I'm getting sick."

"I don't know," she said with a shake of her head. "I haven't been sleeping very well… nightmares, sleepwalking. I keep waking up in weird places."

"I didn't know you were a sleepwalker… that's always creeped me out."

"I didn't know I was a sleepwalker either. You'd think that would be something your mom would tell you, right?"

"Definitely," I said. My mother would have teased me about it mercilessly and if YouTube had been around when I was a kid she definitely would have posted it for the whole world to see.

"I dunno, maybe it's a sign I should buy a ticket home. I'm running out of money... and parental patience."

"Oh, dear," I said with mock sincerity. "Poor lamb, time to go home and get a job."

She sighed heavily and nodded. "Looks like it."

I left Emilie to drown in her misery while I went through the motions of my day. Signore de Sarno was away in Torino for the better part of the week on a lecture tour, which meant I had the archive room to myself, and the freedom to zone out without fear of being discovered. But every noise I heard outside the archive room door made me wonder if it was Aiden—I imagined opening the door to see him standing there with an apology on his lips and a contrite expression on his face, but it never happened.

He may as well have been dead to me, and the dead didn't apologize.

The day dragged, and I waited until the very end of my shift to take my trolley of books up to the mezzanine for re-shelving. The elevator moved even more slowly than usual, and a headache was looming behind my eyes. Every jerky motion of the infernal contraption made my stomach lurch, and I realized that I hadn't eaten lunch. I could barely stand the smell of food, let alone the taste. It had to be that goddamn risotto. I should have known better. "Crackers for dinner," I muttered as the elevator came to a sickening stop. I cranked the doors open and groaned when I saw that it hadn't stopped at the floor, but a few inches above it.

I pulled the trolley out of the elevator carefully, wincing as the antique wheels crashed to the floor under the weight of the books. At least the library would be mostly empty by now so there would be no scolding and tutting from our aged patrons as I pulled the trolley over the threadbare carpets toward the stacks.

The doors to the private meeting rooms were closed, and I tried not to think about the day I'd listened at the door while Signore de Sarno and Aiden had had their meeting. But just the memory of his rumbling voice sent shivers down my spine. I let out a furious breath and pushed the trolley faster, ignoring the squeaking wheel that gave away my presence to anyone nearby.

I started my re-shelving and did my best not to think about Aiden… our last conversation (argument) had been in front of the spiral staircase to my right… I was fooling myself; it was impossible not to think about him and how that strange cold fire had swirled in my chest when we'd kissed, and how it had overtaken me like a blistering inferno when he'd fucked me.

I kicked the trolley wheel. "Stupid."

"Talking to yourself again."

The voice startled me and I almost dropped the books I was balancing in my hurry to see who had spoken. *That's what he'd said to me… on more than one occasion.*

"Emilie, I didn't know you were still here." I looked at my watch and frowned. "It's way past your shift time, you don't have to wait for me."

"It's no trouble, Gideon," she said as she leaned against the railing. Her dark hair had been freed from its usual braids and swung in waves around her shoulders. Her skin was pale, almost sallow, in the dim light and I adjusted my glasses just a little.

"Are you okay? You weren't looking so good when I came in this morning."

"I'm fine," Emilie replied softly. "In fact, I'm feeling much better. But how are you, Gideon?"

I set the book in my hand onto the shelf and shrugged. "The same level of shitty. I'm hungry, but I don't think I can eat anything. I think I caught that flu that's going around… it's just biding its time."

"The flu?" Emilie laughed softly. "Is that what you think it is?"

"What? What else could it be?" I turned around to fix her with a stare, but Emilie wasn't leaning against the railing anymore. I looked around quickly. *Where the hell had she gone?*

The library was silent except for the sound of my heart beating in my ears. This was getting weird. What the hell was going on? This ancient floor creaked when a fly landed on it, how was she doing that?

"How much do you know about mythology, Gideon?" Emilie's voice floated to me from the middle of the room, and I peered around the bookshelf to see her wandering between the map desks, turning off the little reading lamps as she went.

Click.
Click.
Click.

"Uhh... enough, I guess. Why?"

"Doesn't being in a city as ancient as this make you think about it more? Doesn't it make you think these things could have been real? How much easier it would have been to explain thunder and lightning as something created by a god?"

"Sure, I mean, anything is possible. We're also really close to Vatican City, too close if you ask me. They believe the same kind of nonsense over there," I gestured towards the holy city with a careless hand.

"The only difference is, what they believe isn't real..." Emilie's voice was quiet and I leaned around the bookshelf to look at her again. She was staring up at the stained glass skylight in the center of the room, not moving, just staring.

"Whatever you say, Em," I muttered.

"All the myths say that the gods were married—husbands and wives, pledged to each other in the sight of the pantheon. It seems ridiculous doesn't it? That immortal beings should be bound by the rules that mankind placed upon itself." Emilie's voice sounded strange and far away, but I kept shelving my books. The faster I finished, the faster I could leave... and forget this conversation.

"Sure... ridiculous."

"So you agree with me, you agree that there should be different rules for gods and men…" Emilie's face appeared at the edge of the bookshelf, startling me. I tried not to show it, but I was rattled. This was entirely too weird, and my stomach was churning again.

"I mean… if you think about it, it makes sense that the ancients made their gods in their own image… they were married, they followed certain rules. Why shouldn't the gods? They weren't real anyway."

Emilie laughed, and the sound was spiteful instead of joyful and it made my skin crawl. "Is that so?" she said through her laughter. She leaned against the railing again and looked at me carefully, suddenly sober. "But the gods didn't follow the rules, Gideon. They philandered and raped; they seduced and took things that they wanted. Women… men… whatever they pleased. Without repercussion. Zeus alone had over forty children. Forty! Do you think Hera bore all of them?"

I shook my head dumbly. "Em, I'm not sure what you're trying to—"

"I'm trying to tell you that the gods are liars… liars who cannot be trusted to follow the rules. Simple rules, Gideon. Fidelity, honor, respect… these words mean nothing to them."

"Okay…"

"And how many of those children were orphaned, Gideon? Do you know?"

"Orphaned? I don't know…"

"Zeus could escape the wrath of his wife easily; he was divine, just like she was. Untouchable. But the mortals… the mortals were so much easier to deal with. Hera punished her husband in the only way that could touch him, by striking his lovers. Perhaps, she reasoned, he would learn his lesson when the things he wanted were taken away. Like a child. But he didn't learn anything…" Emilie's voice was changing as she spoke, and I noticed for the first time how black her eyes were; like two pools of tar.

She had pushed herself up on the railing, and her feet dangled, swinging lightly. Her heels hit the wrought iron, making a soft chime each time she moved.

"Em, you're making me really nervous," I said as I set down my books. I edged towards her, holding out my hand. "Come on, get down. Let's go get some gelato; I think that'll make my stomach stop doing cartwheels. Come on."

Emilie reached out and grabbed my hand, and I winced as she gripped it tightly between her pale fingers. She took a shuddering breath and stared at me with those deep, black eyes. "Oh, Gideon," she sighed. "I should have known it would be you…"

"What? I've always been here…"

"He's marked you, I can feel it." Her words were gentle, but I could see malice glittering in her eyes, and I felt a chill ripple up my spine.

"Oh, god," I murmured.

"Yes… oh, yes. You thought you were just getting the fuck of a lifetime, didn't you? Tall, dark, and menacing with a hint of sadism… he's everything you've ever wanted, isn't he? And you're everything he's ever wanted, too. You were made for him, Gideon, and you didn't even know it." Emilie's grip tightened on my fingers and I heard something crack.

The ancient hardwood creaked on the floor below and I looked around in a panic, hoping someone else was there. Anyone.

"There's no one here to rescue you, Gideon. In any case, they'll be too late. My mother will be so very pleased that I've found you." She pulled me closer, and held my face in her other hand; her fingertips dug into my cheeks and jaw as she examined me. "I can see why he likes you, I can smell defiance on you. He'll enjoy breaking you, testing you… and you would have tested him." She inhaled deeply and her eyes rolled back in her head. I struggled in her grip. She was insane, that much was clear, and I needed to get the hell away from her.

"Let me go! You're fucked in the head!" I cried as I pulled away, but she held me fast. "You're hurting me!"

"It will be over soon, Gideon," she said. She released my face and trailed her hand down over my chest towards my stomach, and then her eyes widened and she crushed my hand once more. I cried out in pain and tried to twist out of her grip. "Already seeded... my mother will enjoy crushing the life out of you, mortal," she hissed.

With a wild cry I pushed against her with all my strength, and the grip on my hand released as she fell over the railing, an expression of dull surprise on her beautiful alabaster face. I stumbled backwards and fell hard on the wooden floor; I lay there panting, waiting for the sound of her impact and Emilie's cries of pain, but the sickening *thud* I'd been expecting never came.

I scrambled to my feet and ran to the railing. "Emilie!" I shouted her name as I leaned over to look for her crumpled corpse, but the floor of the *Sala Monumentale* was bare and untarnished.

"What the fuck!"

My voice echoed around the room, but before it could die away, it was eclipsed by the sound of laughter: high, cold, and cruel. And then the rushing of whistling wings, as though a thousand ducks had taken flight inside the library. The sound beat against the windows and vibrated the floors, and I could feel the hardwood shaking beneath my feet.

I sank to my knees in disbelief as cracks began to form in the ceiling, and the sound of beating wings became the rumbling of something more... behind me, the stained glass skylight cracked and shattered, spilling colored glass over the map desks. I cried out in alarm as the bookshelves began to sway and then crash to the ground.

The last thing I saw before the roof crashed in was Emilie—but not Emilie at all. A woman with long black hair that writhed in the wind created by the beat of the falcon's wings that had sprouted from her back. She hovered above me as my world came crashing down around my head, and her laughter filled my ears as the *Biblioteca Vallicelliana* crumbled. The floor trembled beneath me, shuddering and shifting. And then all I could see was darkness.

CHAPTER 13 ~ HADES

The dust was thick, and the scream of car alarms and sirens filled the air. Emergency vehicles sped through the narrow, uneven streets and I watched them all with a mixture of horror and anger pulsing through my veins.

The *Biblioteca Vallicelliana* was destroyed. The whole block was destroyed.

"Uncle... what happened?" Hermes appeared behind me and I shook my head in disbelief.

"*Terremoto!*" someone shouted. "Earthquake! Don't go inside, the aftershocks..."

I grabbed the man who had shouted, jerking him off balance. "What else was destroyed? Have there been any casualties?"

My voice was full of anger and desperation. The man's eyes were wide as he stared at me. "No... nothing else," he stammered as I dropped him. "The library was closed... there should have been no one inside. *Per grazia di Dio.*"

When I had looked for Gideon, all I had seen in the cistern was fog. Someone screamed, and there was a *crash* from within the ruined shell of the library. Another cloud of dust crept along the street.

I wasn't going to stand in the street any longer. Gideon was in there.

"Signore! The roof!"

"Fuck the roof," I muttered and ran for the building. The front facade of the ancient buildings had crumbled away, filling the narrow alley with bricks, mortar, and tiles. I scrambled through the debris, passing emergency crews who barely registered my presence. A shadow, moving through the wreckage, nothing more. Hermes followed close behind, blending seamlessly with the fading sunlight to hide from the eyes of the mortals.

The reception desk was crushed, a massive marble column lay across it, impossible to move, the archive room door was closed, and that side of the building seemed curiously untouched by the damage, save for some wide cracks in the plaster walls. Pieces of the ornate ceiling had come away and smashed on the tiled floor. Gideon wasn't here.

"Uncle!"

Hermes was standing on a pile of bricks outside the entrance to the *Sala Monumentale*; his expression was a mixture of pain and worry, and I felt my heart freeze in my chest. He held something out to me— a feather. I snatched it from his fingers and examined it carefully. A flight feather. Longer than any natural feather should be. Pale, and striped with dark brown bars. A hawk... "Eris."

The floor shuddered as I said the goddess' name and Hermes' expression hardened. He had never liked his half-sister, and now he had even less reason to. "Acting on Hera's orders, no doubt," he said bitterly.

"Acting on her own," I replied.

I tucked the feather into my cloak and jumped down the pile of bricks to the ruptured tile floor. It had buckled and rippled with the force of the quake, and loose pieces of tile skidded under my bare feet.

The mezzanine had cracked in half, spilling bookshelves and books down onto the main floor like an avalanche. *There*. A pale hand, protruding from under a fallen bookshelf caught my eye.

"Gideon."

I flung the bookshelves aside with all my godly strength, hurling them against the already ruined walls with enough force to lengthen the cracks in the ceiling. I dug through the books desperately as chunks of plaster and marble rained down around us. Shouts from the emergency crews filled the air and the flashing lights of their vehicles bathed the library in blue and red.

"Hurry!" Hermes' harsh whisper reminded me that other mortals were approaching. They couldn't have Gideon. I was the only one who could save him now. "Is it too late?"

I grabbed Gideon's dirty hand and held it tightly. The cold fire that should have swept through my hand and up my arm only gave me the barest shiver of sensation.

There was no such thing as 'too late' for the god of death.

An aftershock rumbled through the building, shaking loose more plaster. A massive light fixture swung crazily from its chain before the plaster broke free and it plummeted towards us. With the same ease that he had extinguished the fire in my library so many centuries ago, Hermes summoned a gust of wind to push the falling debris aside. The plaster shattered over the floor, scattering shards of glass and ornate fittings across the tile. "She must be close by," he said.

"No doubt she is watching us right now," I snarled.

Wrapping myself in shadow, I pushed aside another cascade of books to reveal Gideon. He lay where he had fallen, one arm curled protectively around his stomach. His blood stained the floor and his glasses were crushed on the tiles. My heart lurched at the sight of him.

The wreckage of the mezzanine shifted and creaked as I pulled Gideon free as gently as I could. I gritted my teeth as he groaned faintly in pain. He was barely alive, and his eyelids fluttered weakly as I cradled him against my chest. My broken mortal.

Eris would pay for this with her immortal life.

The shadows around us deepened as the emergency crews came through the fallen facade, but all they found were Gideon's broken glasses and the smear of his blood on the tiles as I willed us to Olympus and left the mortal world behind.

In a cloud of black smoke, we arrived in Olympus' throne room. Hermes skidded to a stop beside me; his face was a mask of pure panic.

"What are you doing? He can't be here! It doesn't matter if he has the spark of the divine or not, you know the law—no mortal can step foot on Olympus!"

"He's no mortal," I said. I looked down into Gideon's ashen face. "Not anymore."

My nephew blinked at me for just a moment before he reached out and laid his palm against Gideon's cheek. I resisted the urge to flinch away, but it took every ounce of strength I had.

"Dead... but—"

"Get me the ambrosia and meet me at the Gates," I interrupted him swiftly. This was not the time, and I had no patience left.

Hermes nodded his golden head grimly; he knew that place well, and I knew that I could trust him. Of all my divine kin, Hermes was the only one who understood me... as much as I allowed him to.

I held Gideon gently against my chest, as the door that led down to the great gate of the Underworld yawned open in the marble floor beneath my black basalt throne.

I didn't need to take the stairs, but there was something solemn about making this journey to rekindle my spark.

The great black gate had marked the entrance to the Underworld since the fall of our father, Cronos. I had built it myself, full of rage and bitterness while my brothers had created the shining columns of Olympus. If their marble palace was a shrine to their triumph, this gate was a shrine to my hatred.

The red dirt beneath my feet was covered in a soft layer of ash from the volcano that smoked in the heart of Tartarus.

"Are you sure you want to do this?" Hermes was at my side, a small box of glittering black obsidian in his hand.

"You were there when Zeus announced it. When we find our sparks, we'll know." I laid Gideon down on a bed of grey ash and smoothed his dark hair away from his forehead. His face was covered in dust and blood, but a single tear had cut a path through the grime on his cheek. "I've been running from this for too long, and now I'm being punished for it."

"I'll watch over him," Hermes said.

Without a word, I turned away and strode through the gates of the Underworld. The ground rumbled beneath my feet as Tartarus' volcano belched its black smoke.

There was only one way I could take back what had been done.

Acheron, the River of Souls, wound its way through the Underworld in an unending current. I stood on the edge of its dark banks and stared into the water. The glint of coins— bronze, silver, and gold —the fare brought by the dead to guarantee their passage into the Underworld, shone up through the rippling water. Ancient and modern, all who stood on the banks of the Acheron had to pay their way. Gold rings, watches, necklaces—new offerings next to the old. *No one rides for free.*

But there were other things in the water… the souls of the dead, those who could not afford passage to the Underworld, caught for all eternity in the current.

I closed my eyes and waded into the river. The coins slipped beneath my feet, and the shades of the dead spun away from me like startled shoals of skeletal fish. *Gideon.* This was where I would find him. He had come to the Underworld without his fare, and his shade would spin in the current until the world ended.

Deeper, and deeper. One foot in front of the other, I reached out to Gideon with my thoughts and held the image of him in my mind. The way his eyes had flashed as he'd shouted at me in the library. The water tugged at my cloak and the shades of the dead wound around my legs, but still I walked forward. I was drawn farther, responding to something I couldn't explain.

There. Pale and ghostly, caught in the current. The handsome librarian looked gaunt in his shade form.

Gideon.

But it couldn't have been. His hair curled over his forehead in the same way I remembered. Cradled in his arms was a small bundle; and I felt my stomach drop.

A child.

Eris had not only attempted to murder my spark, but my child…

Anger swelled in my chest, and I pushed forward through the water towards him. His shade was oblivious to me, caught in his own misery. His shade bore none of the smudges of grime and mortar dust, but the wound on his head remained. I reached down toward him, and he finally realized that I was there. He flinched away from my hand and cradled the bundle closer to his chest.

"Come now," I murmured, but Gideon floated out of my grasp, his shade winding with the others. "This is no time to be shy."

He had pursued me, now it was my turn to chase him. I pushed aside the shades that hid him from my view and laid my hand on his pale shoulder. But my hand passed through it. I frowned and tried again, but I couldn't touch him.

"Gideon…"

The librarian, my spark, turned his eyes upon me and I could feel the weight of his sadness.

"You were meant to be mine. Come with me, and we can be together. No more lies." Gideon's mouth moved in silent accusation and I shook my head. "How could I tell you that this was real? What I was. It was easier this way… easier to frighten you and pretend it was all just a mistake."

Gideon turned away, and I felt my stomach twist. *He wanted an apology. Was that what it would take?* I gritted my teeth and my hands clenched into fists at my side. The shades of the dead spun around my legs, and a crowd of them had gathered on the far shore. The last thing I wanted was an audience.

"I… I'm the reason this happened to you," I said finally. "It's my fault that Eris found you… I shouldn't have given in."

Gideon's pale gaze burned into mine. *That's not good enough.*

"I couldn't resist not knowing if this prophecy was meant for me," I said through gritted teeth. "And then you… I couldn't resist. My desire for you made me weak, and I put you in danger." I paused and reached for him again, my hand passed through his shade once more, but I could have sworn that there was some substance to his form now. His eyes begged me to say the words.

"I'm sorry," I said softly. There was a murmur from the shades of the dead that were gathered on the shore, and the current seemed to pull at me more strongly. I reached for Gideon again, and this time when my fingers touched his shoulder I felt that burst of cold fire rushing up my arm.

"Say it again," came his reply.

I smiled and pulled him closer. "You drive a hard bargain," I muttered. "I'm sorry," I said louder. "I shouldn't have put you in danger. I will always protect you… and our child." Gideon smiled and I could feel his shade growing more solid under my fingers. The cold fire that had been so faint before flared in my chest, stronger than ever. I gathered Gideon up in my arms and waded out of the river with his shade nestled against my chest.

Hermes had kept guard over Gideon's body, and his face lit up when he saw us approaching. The volcano rumbled in the distance as I knelt in the ash-covered dirt to lay Gideon's shade on top of his body. I held my breath as the shade sank down. Back where it belonged.

Gideon's ashen complexion remained unchanged, and I held out my hand to Hermes. "The ambrosia."

My nephew gave me the shining black box without a word and stood silently as I removed a small piece of the ambrosia and set it between Gideon's slack lips. As soon as the ambrosia touched his tongue, I saw the pallor of his skin begin to change. His cheeks warmed and I heard Hermes let out a long breath.

"Tell the others," I said softly as Gideon's eyelids fluttered and he took a shuddering breath. Hermes was gone in a gust of wind and I pulled Gideon's head into my lap. "Wake up, librarian."

Gideon's eyes opened, dark and shining with a hint of gray that he'd carried with him from the Acheron. "What happened?"

"Something I should have prevented," I said.

Gideon raised his eyebrow and then his expression changed and his hands shot to his stomach. "She said... is it true?"

"Yes."

"But it's impossible..."

"It is possible. But only for you, and precious few others like you." I reached down to drag my fingers through his dark curls. "Considering what you've been through in the last twenty-four hours, it might be time for a little less cynicism. I just dragged you out of the river of the dead; I've broken my own laws because I couldn't go through this immortality without you. All you have to do is say yes."

Gideon considered what I'd said for a moment before looking up at me again. "And if I don't... what happens?"

"What happens? I'll send you back to Rome and your ruined library. The spark of the divine will allow you to carry my child... but it is of Olympus, and will kill you as it grows too fast for your body to adjust." I paused, watching as my words sank in. "Or Eris will come back to finish what she started."

Gideon's hand tightened around his stomach as he considered it. "So I don't have a choice."

"Of course you do, but the alternative isn't exactly ideal."

"No shit," he said quietly. "And if I stay?"

"If you stay, you can take the rest of the ambrosia that re-animated your shade, and I'll take you to Olympus... You'll be mine forever. You will bear my children and I will give you anything you ask for... Rule beside me."

Gideon chuckled. "That sounds too good to be true."

"Does it? You had to die to get here..."

Gideon's smile faded away, and I knew he was thinking about the earthquake, about Eris, and about the gray current that had almost swept him away from me.

"I won't be paraded around like some trophy." He struggled to sit up and fixed me with a stern glare. I laid a hand over my heart and looked at him seriously.

"Not until you're ready," I said.

He nodded, his eyes on the shining stone box that sat on the ground beside me. "I'll stay," he said. "But I'm still mad at you."

I opened the obsidian box and held it out to him. "I hope you'll let me try to make it up to you," I replied.

"We'll see." He reached in and took the ambrosia without hesitating. A small smile twitched at the corners of his mouth before he ate it in one bite. His eyes closed as he savored the taste.

"Pomegranate," he said. "Fitting."

"As long as you plan on sticking around," I said warily.

"We'll see. You have a lot of apologizing to do," he replied tartly.

Instead of taking the bait, I lowered my face to his and claimed his lips in a kiss that I should have indulged in a long time ago; a kiss full of apologies and promises that I would never speak aloud. The tang of pomegranate that lingered on his lips fueled my passion for him, and he gasped against my mouth as the same cold fire that ran through my veins flared in his.

When our kiss finally broke, Gideon looked up at me with his wide, dark eyes, full of trust and something I couldn't name, but that made the fire in my chest surge anew. I pulled Gideon to his feet, and he leaned against me unsteadily. It would take some time for the ambrosia to make its way into his bloodstream, but when it did, he would be immortal, just like Cameron and Brooke.

I held him tightly against my side and willed us to my library. Gideon's gasp of surprise and awe was music to my ears and I smiled as he stumbled forward to run his fingers over the spines of the books on the shelves closest to us.

"I think you'll like it here," I said.

EPILOGUE ~ HERMES

Gideon recovered slowly, slower than any of us could have anticipated. Apollo assured us that the child in his belly was unharmed, but Gideon had been instructed to rest. My uncle had taken those words to heart, and he kept Gideon secreted away in his library lair for longer than was probably necessary. But the mortal seemed content in his new role as the consort of Hades—most often I found him curled in a chair by the fire in the library with a book on his lap and Cerberus laying at his feet.

Brooke's pregnancy was advancing, and the shy young man had overcome some of his trepidation as he adjusted to life on Olympus. Cameron was, as I had expected, a worthy match for my father. He was pure and excitable, and his presence put a smile on the face of anyone who crossed his path.

Alkira, the newly born Goddess of the Spring Winds was just beginning to toddle unsteadily around the airy nursery when Hades brought Gideon to Olympus. She was growing quickly, and it wouldn't be long before we would all be chasing her through the marble halls of the divine palace.

My father had been changed by the birth of this child. She represented so much more than just the fulfillment of a prophecy. Gideon's death at the hands of my sister, Eris, had opened a deep wound in Zeus' heart, but it was Ares who gave me the most cause for concern.

My stoic brother had been the only one in the throne room when I had returned from the Underworld.

He had been staring into the cistern, seated on his red sandstone throne when I appeared.

"Brother, I have news."

"Don't you always," he had replied, disinterested in my sudden appearance.

"Our uncle, Hades, has brought his spark back to Olympus... he was almost killed by Eris..."

"And the child?"

"They both live," I said. "Even now he will be taking the ambrosia and will join the pantheon at our uncle's side."

Ares had nodded and looked back into the cistern, but when I stepped closer he swept his hand over the surface, obscuring the view with thick clouds.

"Good... The children are the key to the survival of Olympus. I know how important this prophecy is to our father. Hades' capitulation is an unexpected occurrence." Ares stepped down from his throne and strode towards me. "You will want to tell the others. I believe you'll find father in the nursery."

And then he was gone, in a flash of hot wind, and I blinked in confusion.

I had never known my brother to take much interest in anything our father did, and I wondered if he held any bitterness towards these new immortals... I had struggled with my own jealousy—I doubted our father had ever looked down on our sleeping forms the way he watched his new daughter. I doubted he had ever held a lover as tenderly as he did Cameron.

I walked to the edge of the throne room and looked out at the clouds that shrouded Olympus from mortal eyes.

When he had brought Cameron to Olympus, Zeus had urged all of us to find our own sparks—there was one for each of us. But I could not face the thought of failing in my own search. I could not watch another mortal die in my arms because of this curse. And after seeing Gideon's ashen face, cold to the touch, I could not put my spark in danger.

The goddesses were growing bolder in their attacks and I didn't know what I would do if something happened to my spark. If I ever found them...

I heard footsteps on the marble floor and turned to see my father striding towards me. "Hades has returned with his spark? Is it true?"

"Yes, father. But the goddesses... the attempt on his life. They almost succeeded. But Hades brought his shade back from Acheron—"

"Hades broke his own law."

I nodded. "My uncle sent me away after Gideon was revived. He's already pregnant, father. Another New Olympian."

Zeus nodded thoughtfully. "Good," he said, and then laid a heavy hand upon my shoulder. "You have been away from Olympus for some time, my son. What *have* you been doing?" He raised an eyebrow and observed me carefully, and I tried not to flinch.

"Doing? I've been doing my job, father. The mortals might have changed the way they see us, but it doesn't change anything else."

"Do you know where Hera is?" he said suddenly.

My eyes widened and I tried to quiet the flare of panic in my chest. "No, father... of course not. I would tell you immediately if I knew."

Zeus nodded and looked out over the clouds. "You've been too cavalier, my son. We are at war and *you* are walking a very fine line. Hera will never stop. You know this as well as I do. What will it take to make you choose a side?"

I shook my head and shifted uncomfortably. "I don't know what you're talking about," I said quickly. "My duty is to you, and Olympus... you know that."

"See that you keep it that way," Zeus said quietly.

"Of course, father."

He stood beside me for several minutes, silent and still, as though he were carved from the same marble as the columns that rose around us. I stayed as still as I could, but my body vibrated with the need to run as far away from this place as fast as I could. Without another word, I willed myself to earth and left my father standing on the edge of Olympus, staring down over the mortal world. I only hoped he wasn't watching me.

To Be Continued in *Swift Wings - New Olympians, Book 4*

ABOUT THE AUTHOR

C. J. Vincent is a new author of M/M romance and MPREG.
Mythology + LGBT = <3

Website

ALSO BY C. J. VINCENT

New Olympians

Lightning Strikes ~ Zeus

Rip Tide ~ Poseidon

By the Book ~ Hades

Swift Wings ~ Hermes

Marble Heart ~ Ares

Eternal Flame ~ Hephaestus

BOX SET (All 6 Books + Holiday Novella)

Printed in Great Britain
by Amazon